Gone Away

By Bonnie Dee

ISBN: 978-1-45645-055-7
Copyright © 2010

All rights reserved. Without limiting the rights under copyright reserved above, no part of this publication may be reproduced, stored in or introduced into a retrieval system, or transmitted, in any form, or by any means (electronic, mechanical, photocopying, recording, or otherwise) without the prior written permission of both the copyright owner and the above publisher of this book.

This is a work of fiction. Names, characters, places, brands, media, and incidents are either the product of the author's imagination or are used fictitiously. The author acknowledges the trademarked status and trademark owners of various products referenced in this work of fiction, which have been used without permission. The publication/use of these trademarks is not authorized, associated with, or sponsored by the trademark owners.

Bone Deep

BONNIE DEE

CHAPTER ONE

Discordant carnival music and the smell of burnt sugar, popcorn and axle grease drifted through the crisp fall air. In the dusk, the colored lights of the rusty rides shone in broken lines where bulbs were missing. Faded canvas tents housed games of chance, a fortune-teller, a fun house and freaks. Sarah walked the trash-strewn paths between booths and rides and wondered why she'd come. She hated carnivals.

"Sarah, you made it!" Grace May called across the loud music and barker's cries. She caught up with Sarah and linked arms. "I'm so glad. You spend far too much time alone on the farm. You need to get out more."

Sarah smiled without comment. It was easy to read Grace's message between the lines. 'Stop grieving. John was killed over a year and a half ago. It's time to start living again.' But Grace couldn't possibly know what Sarah felt like inside, hard as drought-baked earth longing for rain but more likely to shed water than soak it in and grow soft again. John's body had been shipped home from the front just before V.E. day ended the war. She could pinpoint April 29, 1945 as the day her heart froze. The moment she'd seen John in the coffin and realized his death was real, Sarah had stopped feeling much of anything.

She drew her light blue cardigan more tightly around her. There was a chill in the air at the end of a hot September day.

Grace squeezed her arm. "Look, I know you're going to be mad at me but—"

"Grace, what'd you do?"

"I told Mike to bring a friend along. You know Andrew Harper, who works at the hardware store? He's new in town, single, almost forty but a real sweet guy and he's looking for someone."

"Well, I'm not." Sarah pulled her arm away from Grace, annoyed at her friend's meddling. "And I don't appreciate your match-making without consulting me first."

"Come on. Don't be upset. It's only for this one evening. If you don't like the guy, you don't have to see him again. Oh look, there they are." Grace grabbed Sarah's arm again and tugged her toward two men standing near the entrance to one of the tents.

Grace's husband, Mike, was talking to a red-haired guy with a pleasant smile on his freckled face. He wore a short-sleeved shirt and a navy blue sweater-vest, and she vaguely remembered seeing the man when she had her screen door repaired at McNulty's Hardware. She might even have talked to him, but if she had, it hadn't left an impression.

Harper's grip was warm and his smile shy as he shook her hand. "Hi. I'm Andrew Harper. I work at—"

"McNulty's. I know. I've seen you there. I'm Sarah

Cassidy." She pulled her hand away from his and adjusted her sweater around her shoulders, aware of Grace and Mike exchanging glances. "So, how do you like living in Fairfield?"

Harper shifted on his feet and a flush crept up from his neck, covering his freckles. "I like it just fine." He cleared his throat and looked across the fairgrounds.

"That's nice." Sarah couldn't think of a single thing to add. She didn't want to make small talk. She wished she was at home reading a book or listening to the radio.

Mike stepped forward interrupting, the awkward moment. "How about a ride on the Ferris wheel, ladies?"

"Not for me," Grace replied. "I hate heights and even if I didn't I wouldn't trust that thing." She indicated the ancient metal wheel arching against the night sky. The cars swayed as it jerked to a stop.

"How about in here?" Andrew pointed to the tent near them.

The painting on the side of the canvas showed obese, bearded, dwarfed, misshapen, tattooed, hermaphrodite freaks. You could gawk at them for only a quarter. She thought those who were willing to pay to view handicapped people were more pathetic than the unfortunates themselves. But Grace and Mike agreed so Sarah paid her money and followed the others inside.

In the hushed darkness beneath the canvas, each display was illuminated by a single bare bulb. The dim light cast odd shadows, adding to the gloomy atmosphere of the stifling tent. Heat from earlier in the day was trapped in the airless enclosure. The smell of unwashed bodies and cow manure was rank.

Sarah removed her cardigan and tied it around her hips. Only a few other people wandered from one attraction to the next. There was a placard set up in front of each 'display'. There was a calf with a fifth leg lying on a bed of straw. A two-foot-tall dwarf sat on a stool, smoking a cigarette and gazing impassively at the fair-goers. Sarah felt as if she'd stepped back into medieval times as she trailed her friends from one mistake of nature to the next. What next? Bear baiting and a public execution?

She watched the bearded woman open her robe to reveal a breast then tug on her facial hair to prove its validity. Feeling like a voyeur, Sarah dropped her gaze. She moved on to observe another woman who had some kind of growth on the side of her neck, which on closer examination proved to have stunted facial features--nature's aborted attempt at a twin.

The others lingered, studying the woman with the tumor, but Sarah moved quickly ahead, anxious to be out of the hot, oppressive tent. It felt wrong to be gaping at these peoples' anomalies.

The next station appeared to be empty. The wooden chair beneath the yellow glow of the light bulb was empty. Sarah peered into the shadows behind the spotlighted chair and saw something moving. Then the dark figure stepped into the circle of light.

Sarah drew in her breath.

The man was a walking tapestry of color. Every bit of his skin was covered in tattoos. Angels, devils, dragons, flames, flowers and skulls were tossed on blue waves. There was no common theme to the tattoos and only the decorative blue swirls connected them. It gave the impression of flotsam floating in the wake of a shipwreck.

In the center of the man's chest was a red heart, not a Valentine confection but a knobby fist-shaped lump with stubs of aortas sticking out. Wrapped around the heart were links of black chain, binding it tight. The movements of his muscles as he took his seat caused the images to expand and contract, as if they pulsed with life.

With all the ink covering his body, it took Sarah a moment to notice how very nearly naked he was. A loincloth hung from his hips. As he sat, propping one knee up on a rung of the chair, the cloth opened to reveal that his thigh was covered with images right up to his groin.

A flush of heat lanced through her, settling warmly in between her legs. She brushed her hair back from her burning cheeks and tucked it behind her ear. She knew she should move on, but couldn't stop staring at the tattooed man.

He gazed past her, across the tent, focusing on something. Sarah fought the urge to look over her shoulder at whatever he was seeing.

His body was as concealed as if he were clothed. The designs covered every limb and muscle, distracting the eye from his nudity. Even his face and shaven head were tattooed. More tentacles of the swirling blue design marked his cheeks and framed his eyes making their vivid blue seem to glow like a gas flame. When he turned his head to the side, images bloomed up the back of his neck and fanned over his scalp in a fountain of colors. The shreds of pale skin between the tattoos served as contrast to red, purple, ochre, green and inky black.

Sarah suddenly realized that her friends had already looked at the tattooed man and gone on ahead while she still stood and stared. Unwillingly, she started to walk away. Just then he turned his head and his eyes caught and held Sarah's.

Her breath stopped and her heart pounded. He was gazing at her as intently as she had been looking at him, peering deep inside her.

She felt naked in front of him and longed to run away from his searing gaze, but found it impossible to move her feet. It was as if he saw and marked her pain, still percolating underneath the veneer of dull ennui. His scalpel gaze hurt as it cut through her scars. Tears stung her eyes and she blinked to clear them.

Then the man looked away, once again staring sightlessly at that invisible mark on the opposite side of the tent.

Sarah moved on, feeling shaken and anxious, wondering what had just happened. That moment of connection had been as sharp and real as anything she'd ever experienced. She longed to go home, bury herself under her bedcovers, and forget what she'd seen tonight.

She hurried past the rest of the exhibits, but before she followed her friends out of the sideshow Sarah took a last glance at the tattooed man. A cluster of people blocked her view. She had to leave without seeing him again.

The rest of the evening passed in a blur of carnival lights and music and too much noise. She made pointless small talk with Grace, Mike, and Andrew but nothing registered. She felt as if she was walking in a dream. Her mind kept returning to the arresting vision of the tattooed man, to his intense eyes even more than the art decorating his muscular body. If only she could steal away from her friends, pay her quarter and see him one last time. Instead, she bid them all goodnight, rejected Andrew's offer to see her home, and walked over the hill, through the pasture to her house.

Lying in bed, she stared out the window at the stars and mused that the images on the skin of the tattooed man were like the constellations, unrelated picture-stories joined together in glittering array.

When she finally slept, she had strange, erotic dreams. There were no stories, only lust-drenched sensations and provocative images. She saw the Virgin Mary and a grinning, horned devil coiled in an embrace and when she reached out to touch them she felt hot skin beneath her palms.

She awoke gasping for breath, wet between the legs and her nipples hard with arousal. Sweat dampened her hair and molded her nightgown to her body. She steadied her breath until it was back under control, then rose and shook out her twisted sheet. With the covers smoothed, she lay down again and tried to sleep, but images of colorful skin continued to tease her imagination. Her own skin ached and burned as if she had a fever, especially where her thighs pressed together. At last, she pulled off her nightgown and tossed it on the floor.

When she closed her eyes, the tattooed man was staring back at her. She caressed her breasts, pulling and rolling her nipples between her fingers. She slipped a hand between her legs and touched herself delicately at first, then moving her finger in rapid circles over her clitoris. Sparks of pleasure exploded in colorful bursts and she gave a quiet moan, arching up toward the sky before tumbling down onto sweat-damp sheets.

Afterward, she stared at the ceiling, following the crack in the plaster that traveled across the south corner of the room. For a moment, the release of tension left her feeling better, more like herself. But when she closed her eyes again, the tattooed man was *still* looking at her.

After another hour of fruitlessly pursuing sleep, Sarah rose, dressed, and went outside. The chill, pre-dawn air filled her lungs like ice and slapped her wide awake. Stiff, frost-covered grass crunched underfoot as she walked across the pasture and over the hill once more.

The field below was empty, trampled, muddy and trash-strewn. Deep ruts led from up a dirt track to the road. The carnival had moved on, but the memory of the tattooed man lingered. She felt as if something precious had been snatched away from her, like the brass ring on a carnival ride always just out of reach.

But it wasn't as if she could've gone down there anyway, sought out the tattooed man and introduced herself. "Hi there. My name's Sarah. Let's talk."

Exhausted and drained, she turned and trudged on leaden legs back to the farm.

CHAPTER TWO

By the time she reached home, the sun was up. She made coffee and listened to the morning news on the radio, then went out to the barn to milk the cow and feed the horse. She missed Sheba plodding along at her side. The old dog had died the previous winter and Sarah hadn't had the heart to replace her. Sheba had been John's childhood pet and Sarah's last link with her husband. To get a new pup felt like a betrayal. She wasn't ready for it, but the place was lonely without a pet.

Inside the barn she filled the water troughs for the livestock and put grain in Edison's feedbox. She patted the horse's velvet nose. He huffed a warm breath from his huge nostrils before dipping his head to eat.

Sarah forked out the dirty hay from both stalls then stopped to milk Millie before pitching down fresh hay from the loft. Millie gave her only a half pail of milk. Maybe she could put the cow in with Bill Peters's herd for a while to mate with his bull. Millie needed to calve again in order to start producing more milk.

After covering the pail and setting it aside, Sarah

climbed the ladder to the haymow. The sweet scent of dry hay tickled her nose and made her sneeze. She jabbed the pitchfork into a pile of hay.

Something moved. Something much bigger than the occasional rat Sarah roused from the straw. A man scrambled away from the pitchfork and leaped to his feet.

Sarah screamed and jumped back. She felt the edge of the loft beneath her foot and empty space beyond it. She dropped the pitchfork as she teetered on the edge, arms waving. The man lunged for her, grabbed her arm and pulled her back from the edge. Then he put a hand over her mouth to silence her screams.

She bit his palm and twisted in his grasp. He jerked his hand free with a wordless cry, released her arm and backed away.

The tattooed man from the carnival stood in her barn loft, hands raised as if she was the sheriff in some Western come to arrest him. He wore black pants and shoes and a navy wool coat to which hay clung, but the colors blooming on his hands and head made him look like some nightmare creature come to life. The strangest part was that he remained utterly silent. He hadn't cursed when she bit him nor did he try to calm her or explain his presence. He stood gazed at her solemnly like he would wait all day until she gave him permission to move.

Sarah's hand went to her chest, covering her racing heart. "What...?" She couldn't find any more words.

The man remained frozen in place.

"You may put your hands down."

He slowly lowered them to his sides.

"Why are you here?" She waited for an answer but he gave none. "Can you speak?"

"Yes." It was a quiet murmur, but so deep it seemed to reverberate through the loft.

She was relieved. She'd been afraid if he wasn't mute he might be so mentally deficient he couldn't understand her.

"What are you doing here?" she asked again.

"Sleeping."

"You've left the carnival? Why?" *Escaped*, her mind whispered.

He remained silent, but his gaze continued to lock onto hers. His eyes were the saddest she'd ever seen. She clenched her hands. Logic told her to dive for the pitchfork or run for the ladder, but his demeanor was non-threatening. She couldn't believe this man was dangerous.

"Did they mistreat you there?" She felt foolish asking. He was a grown man who'd probably chosen to leave unsatisfactory employment, so why did she have images of cages and beatings in her mind?

His jaw tightened, making the blue swirls undulate and, almost imperceptibly, he inclined his head.

"Oh." Her eyes widened as a thought struck. "Will they come looking for you?"

"Maybe."

She moved toward him. "We should go to the police."

He shook his head, backing up a step. "No."

"But were you held against your will? For how long?"

"Always."

"Always." She repeated, trying to comprehend it. "Always? You were raised there?"

"Yes."

"Good God." Sarah had no idea what to say or do next so she said the first thing that popped into her mind, the easy way to make things better. "Are you hungry? Do you want something to eat? Come to the house and I'll make you breakfast."

He nodded.

As she climbed down the ladder, Sarah realized she had just invited this stranger into her home. But the idea of this meek man attempting to hurt her seemed ridiculous. She was struck by the strangeness of the situation. People supposedly ran away to join the circus. Who could imagine a real-life circumstance where someone would be running from it?

The man climbed silently and gracefully down the ladder. As she waited for him at the bottom, she noticed how worn the soles of his shoes were and how threadbare his pants and jacket. He looked like a well-used scarecrow.

They walked across the yard together, and she watched him from the corner of her eye, fascinated by the flames that followed the line of his jaw.

He glanced over and his eyes met hers. Sarah quickly looked away, embarrassed to be caught staring. She opened the back door and scraped her feet off on the mat in the mud room before going inside. She took off her coat and hung it on the hook before she realized the man hadn't followed her. He stood on the bottom step, waiting.

She reached out a hand as if coaxing a wild animal. "It's all right. You can come in."

He brushed at the hay clinging to his coat and looked down at his muddy shoes.

"Take off your coat and hang it, and you can leave your shoes in the entry."

Slowly he walked up the steps, unbuttoning and removing the coat. The long-sleeved, blue cotton shirt he wore underneath was thin with age and ripped at several of the seams. Sarah caught a glimpse of bright colored skin through the gaps in the fabric before she ushered him into the kitchen.

"Please, sit down." She indicated the metal kitchen table covered by a red-flowered oilcloth. Matching metal chairs upholstered in faded red vinyl were gathered around it. Chairs she'd once hoped would be filled by children, but which would continue to remain empty now.

"Eggs and bacon?" She pulled a skillet from the cupboard and set it on the stove.

The silence as she moved around the kitchen preparing breakfast was awkward. She wished her guest would say something—anything. She laid bacon in the skillet.

As it started to sizzle, she leaned against the counter, arms folded, and looked at the stranger. "What's your name?"

He'd been staring at the floor, and looked up as if startled to be addressed. Again she was struck by the vivid blue eyes in that exotic face.

"Tom."

"I'm Sarah." She worried her lower lip. "Can you tell me more about yourself, why you left the carnival, where you're planning on going?"

He studied the linoleum again and didn't reply.

"You don't have any idea where you're going," she guessed.

"No."

The bacon sizzled louder and its rich aroma filled the room.

Sarah stared at the faded linoleum squares—the ones she'd wanted to replace but could never afford to. She thought about the changes she'd never made to John's family home during the four years of her marriage. It wasn't the farmers' way to destroy anything that wasn't completely worn out, but sometimes a person just wanted to break routine and do something new. She drew a deep breath and made an impulsive decision. "I have some odd jobs that need doing around here. You could do them in exchange for meals and a bed in the loft."

He frowned, scanning her face as though trying to read it. "Why? Why would you help me?"

Memories of the previous night's dreams and fantasies tumbled through her mind and she threw them into a closet and firmly shut the door. "Because... I don't know. Because you need help, I guess."

Not wanting to really examine the why at all, she turned to crack a pair of eggs into the bacon grease. A quick glance at Tom as she threw the shells away caught him studying her, and a flush of heat raced through her body. Immediately, Tom looked away. Underneath the swirls of blue, she was sure he was blushing.

She focused her attention on setting the table and serving breakfast. She slid a plate laden with toast, bacon and eggs in front of her guest and watched in shock as he grabbed the spoon, hunched over the plate and scooped one of the eggs into his mouth. He snapped it up like a hungry dog and swallowed it down. He jammed bacon and toast into his mouth as if it might be taken away if he didn't hurry. His jaws bulged. The flames and swirls flowed with his muscles. In less time than it had taken her to crack open one of the eggs, he'd finished the meal.

"Do you want more? I can make you another couple eggs."

He wiped his mouth on the back of his hand and looked up at her with a doubtful frown. "Yeah?"

She smiled. "Of course you can have more. It'll only take a minute."

Twenty minutes later, he polished his plate for the last time. He'd eaten a half dozen eggs, four pieces of toast and eight strips of bacon plus two full glasses of orange juice.

Sarah poured a cup of coffee for each of them then sat down at the table. She asked Tom a few more questions about himself and the carnival but only got monosyllables or silence in answer. She sipped her coffee and tried to think how to draw him out. Perhaps the best thing to put him at ease would be for her to tell him a little about herself.

"This was actually my husband's family farm. It's been in the Cassidy family for three generations, but John and I never got around to making a fourth." She added the words that still stuck in her throat, "He was killed in the war."

She waited for the obligatory "I'm sorry," but he simply watched her with his strange eyes.

"Since John's parents had already passed on, I inherited the farm. I rent out the fields to some of the neighbors. My hands are full just taking care of the three acres around the house, the garden and the animals. It's not really a one-person job, and there are things I'm simply not strong enough to tend to. I'd really appreciate having a handyman around for a few days." She knew she was talking too loud and too fast, but his penetrating stare and utter foreignness made her extremely nervous. "Look, I don't know what happened to you, what those people did, but if you want, we can drive into town and go to the police."

He started to rise. "No." A stench of body odor made her nose crinkle. She'd been too alarmed to register it when he grabbed her arm to keep her from falling from the loft, and the scent of frying bacon had covered the earthy odor until now. She tried to think of a polite way to offer him a bath.

"All right. No police." She set down her cup. "I need to get started on my daily chores. I never did get the hay pitched down for the stock's bedding. If you'd care to do that..."

He appeared relieved and nodded. He stood and picked up his empty plate and cup. "Thank you for the food."

"You're welcome. You can put those in the sink." She watched him move about her kitchen with a sense of astonishment that this was actually happening. This was like a bizarre dream from which she'd soon wake. But when Tom turned and looked at her, she knew this was no dream. She couldn't imagine a man like him if she tried.

Sarah led her house guest to the barn and set him to work pitching hay while she took the horse and cow to the pasture. After that, she showed him her vegetable patch and explained which leaves were weeds. She left him working the rows with a hoe and went to the house to start laundry. At the door she stood and watched him for a moment.

Tom seemed totally content in the task--or maybe he was simply used to following orders. He chopped carefully around each plant. The hot sun beat down and after a moment he stopped to remove his shirt and toss it down at the end of a row. The peacock hue of his skin shone over the rippling muscles of his back and shoulders.

Sarah's stomach fluttered. Yet another wave of heat lightning flashed through her body. Her pulse beat between her legs. She hadn't felt anything like this since John's last leave, that time they'd crashed together as if trying to fool themselves into believing they wouldn't have to part again.

The memory of her dead husband quickly doused the surge of arousal. She hurried into the house and set about doing her chores.

Sarah hated laundry day. She supposed she should be grateful John's father had installed indoor plumbing so she had both hot and cold running water. The update hadn't taken place all that many years ago. But even with that convenience, scrubbing the clothes, running them through the press, rinsing and running them through a second time, was exhausting. An hour later she emerged from the house with a basket full of sheets and undergarments to hang on the line.

Over in the garden Tom was crouched down weeding by hand. She was about to call him to take a break and offer him some refreshment, when the sound of an engine coming up the dirt road caught her attention. A dented, gray pickup truck pulled into the driveway, and when she glanced back at the garden, Tom had disappeared.

The truck parked in front of the house. Sarah set down her laundry basket on the porch and walked toward it, anticipating another interruption to her quiet life.

A man with striking silver-streaked black hair and a full moustache got out of the truck. He was tall and thin, dressed in a black suit, shiny with age. He approached her with a smile that seemed somehow more sinister than friendly--maybe because she had a good idea who he was.

"Good day, ma'am." He offered Sarah his hand. It was damp and clammy, and she had the urge to wipe her hand on her apron after touching it.

"My name is Art Reed, owner of Reed's Entertainments. Maybe you stopped by our show sometime in the past couple of days." He jerked a thumb in the direction of the recently departed carnival.

Sarah folded her arms and tried to appear casual. "Yes, I did. Just last night."

"I hope you enjoyed it. The problem is one of our people has gone missing. I'm canvassing the area to see if anyone has seen him."

"Gone missing?"

Reed shook his head, his moustache drooping as his smile disappeared. "Wandered off most likely. Poor Tom's soft in the head and needs to be looked after. We were twenty miles down the road before I noticed he was gone. He's like my own son. I must find him and get him home safe."

Sarah frowned. "Oh, that's terrible. What does he look like?"

He smiled again, revealing uneven yellow teeth. "You couldn't miss him--the tattooed man, one of our best attractions."

"Yes, I saw him. I mean, at the carnival last night." She stretched her acting skills, widening her eyes and putting her hand over her heart. "Good heavens, is he dangerous?"

"No, not at all. But he's never been on his own. His mother was our fortune-teller and when she died I raised the child. This young man has no idea of how to survive alone, so you can see I must get him safely back to his home."

"Of course, Mr. Reed, I'll keep my eyes open." She shuddered extravagantly. "And my doors locked just in case he's not as harmless as you think. Have you notified the police?"

"Mrs...?"

"Cassidy."

"Mrs. Cassidy, in my business we prefer to take care of things on our own. The authorities aren't always friendly to the traveling entertainment industry. So, if you see Tom I'll be staying at the Fairfield Motel for a night. You can reach me at their phone." He handed her a small piece of paper with a number scrawled on it.

Sarah nearly shuddered as she took it from his bony fingers.

"Tomorrow I must catch up with the carnival over in Hooperstown." He sighed. "I certainly hope I find Tom before I have to leave. I hate to think of the poor imbecile wandering the countryside lost."

"I'll certainly let you know if I see him."

He climbed back into his vehicle and she watched him drive away. After the dust on the road settled, she walked over to the garden. The leaves of dry corn stalks, stripped of their ears this late in the season, whispered together. She knew Tom was in there somewhere, or maybe lying between the rows of bush beans.

"He's gone. You can come out now."

She couldn't help but smile when he popped up in the middle of her garden like some bizarrely painted animal. He rose from between the staked bean plants, brushing dirt off his chest and stomach. It mixed with sweat and streaked him in muddy brown that dulled the vibrant colors.

"Why don't you come inside for a while, out of the hot sun. It's time for a break anyway."

He looked at her for a silent moment, and Sarah was suddenly afraid that Reed's story was true, that this man was mentally feeble and should be reunited with his guardian.

"Thank you," he finally said.

She smiled. "No problem."

His eyes roamed over her eyes, her hair and rested on her mouth until her lips tingled. He didn't return her smile. She wondered if he was even capable of it.

In the kitchen, she offered him a plate of cookies and

lemonade and was again aware of his ripe odor. "Maybe after you eat you'd like to cool down with a bath?"

He looked up at her, cheeks full of cookie, and nodded.

Sarah sat at the table across from him, sipping her drink. "That man Reed says he's your guardian and that you've never lived outside the carnival."

Tom swallowed and washed the cookies down with a huge gulp of lemonade. "Yes."

"Look, if we're going to get anywhere, I need more than yes and no answers from you. Please tell me why this man is after you. What does he want from you?"

There was a pause before Tom spoke, "I'm part of his show. He made me for it."

Sarah had a sudden vision of Frankenstein's monster in that Boris Karloff movie and she shivered. She gestured to Tom's arm. "Did he do all those?"

Tom stretched out his forearm across the table and flexed it, making the angel's wings move. "Yes. Starting with this." He presented his shoulder to her, pointing to a faded red heart with 'Mom' emblazoned in script across it. "When my mother died."

Sarah frowned. "How old were you?"

"Eight."

She swallowed, horrified. "And how old are you now?"

"I don't know."

She couldn't fathom it. How could someone not know his own age? It would mean years drifting by timeless and unmeasured, not counted out by birthday celebrations,

Christmases or any of the special events that humans used to create a semblance of order in their lives. "Were you kept a prisoner then?"

He ran his hand up and down the side of the empty lemonade glass. "Not at first. There was nowhere else to go. But later, when I was older, I wanted to leave so he locked me in my room between shows."

"Did he beat you?"

"No." He held up his hands, indicating his body, and gave a small smile--the first she'd seen on his face. "It would spoil the art."

Sarah's heart ached. Reed may not have beaten this man, but he'd clearly half-starved him, cut him off from human companionship and poked him with needles on a regular basis. There were many ways to torture a person.

"When I saw you at the sideshow, you weren't restrained. Why didn't you simply leave during a show? Walk away some night?"

Tom looked at her with his penetrating eyes. "Where would I go? Where else would I fit in?"

"But you did leave. Last night. What finally gave you the courage?"

"You. You came, just like in my dream."

His words chilled her and warmed her at the same time. His husky voice tickled her spine like a trailing finger and she shivered.

Choosing to ignore his explanation, she drew a deep breath. "Look, it's been a long morning. I'll draw you a bath, find some of my husband's old clothes you can wear, then I need to hang my laundry out to dry. Please lie down in the spare bedroom and take a rest after you've cleaned up."

He nodded.

Sarah led him upstairs and started the bath water running then showed him to John's childhood room. The Cassidys had never changed the room and when John and Sarah moved here, it had been straight into the master bedroom. They'd planned to make the room a nursery, but the need had never arisen.

The dresser was cluttered with baseball trophies and ship models. Pennants and nautical art decorated the walls. The room was a mix of John as a young boy and as a sports-minded teenager. After his death Sarah had intended to clean out the room, donate his old toys, models and clothes to some charity. But every time she walked in here and imagined him sitting at his desk at age twelve, cowlick waving as he carefully painted one of his models, she couldn't bear to go through his possessions.

She got clothes from the dresser, critically eyeing the trousers and then Tom. "John wore these before he went into the service and gained weight. They might fit you."

Tom stood in the center of the room turning in a slow circle, studying everything. He walked over to the bookcase and touched the spines of some of the books.

"You can look through those if you want. Maybe you'll find something interesting to read."

Sarah ushered him toward the bathroom down the hall. She gave him the pile of clothes, a towel, washcloth and John's old shaving kit. "I guess that's everything you'll need.

Leave your dirty clothes on the floor and I'll take them to the laundry room."

Before she'd finished speaking Tom was already taking off his shirt.

She closed the door behind her, then stood in the hallway listening to the rustling clothes and the splash of water as he stepped into the bath. She pictured him totally nude but not, his skin hidden by the designs. She wondered whether tattoos covered every inch of him, even the private parts, and what those parts looked like. Her imaginings aroused an ache in her own privates. She shook her head and forced herself to walk away from the door.

After hanging sheets on the line, she stood in the sunshine and gazed across the yard, listening to the snap of the sheets in the breeze. Suddenly the enormity of what she was undertaking hit her. She had a stranger in her house this very moment using her bathroom, wearing her husband's old clothing and sleeping in his childhood bed. He was strange looking, strange acting, and being pursued by a very strange and frightening man.

How long could she hide Tom and look after him? It was an impossible situation. But what else could she do? Turn him over to the local sheriff to deal with? She could imagine the level of sensitivity to his plight Tom would receive.

She picked up the empty laundry basket and returned to the house. Listening up the stairs, she heard no noise and assumed he was taking a nap as she'd suggested.

The rest of the afternoon Sarah worked through her list

of chores, but she was constantly aware of the stranger's presence in her home.

At almost seven o'clock, Sarah pushed a tray of biscuits in the oven and gave the stew bubbling on the stove a last stir. She glanced at the clock. Tom hadn't stirred all afternoon. She didn't know if he was still asleep or if he thought he must wait in the room until she came to get him. Knowing his odd circumstances, it might be the latter.

She went upstairs and knocked lightly at the door.

"Yes?" His muffled voice came from inside.

"May I ... come in?"

"Yes."

She opened the door to find him sitting on the floor surrounded by books. A child's illustrated volume of fairytales lay open on his lap. He looked up at her, almost smiling. His hand spread over the colored illustration. "I know this."

She bent to look. It was a scene from The Little Mermaid. The mermaid was attempting to walk on her new legs with feet that felt as if they were stepping on broken glass. "Oh, I hate this story. It's so sad. She dies at the end and the prince never knew she was the one who saved his life."

He looked back down at the page, his fingertips caressing it. "My mother told me this story. I didn't know there were pictures."

She sat beside him. "You didn't have books growing up?"

He shook his head and closed the book. He began to straighten the strewn books into piles. Sarah helped.

"Can you read?" she asked.

"Some words."

"Maybe after we have dinner, I can read some of these other stories for you."

"Yes." He looked up at her and this time there was no doubt he was smiling, maybe not with his mouth, but definitely with his shining eyes.

"Come on. Let's eat." She rose and offered a hand to pull him to his feet. She grasped the hand with the orange and yellow sun flaring across the back and it was as if she'd touched the real sun. Her skin sizzled as it slid against his. The moment he was on his feet, she quickly pulled free. His maleness and his body heat overwhelmed her. It was too potent. *He* was too potent. She backed away.

Tom's almost-smile disappeared. His brow furrowed and his fingers curled around where hers had been.

Regaining her composure, Sarah cleared her throat and led the way downstairs.

Tom sat at the table and she dished him up a bowl of beef stew. This time, when he bent his face almost to the bowl and started to shovel the food into his mouth she said softly, "Tom."

He glanced up.

"You can slow down. There's no hurry and there's plenty to eat."

He looked from his half empty bowl to her almost full one and sat up straight, dipping his spoon and taking a careful bite. Sarah felt bad for saying anything, but if he was embarrassed he didn't show it.

After they'd eaten dinner and tidied the kitchen, they

settled in the living room.

Sarah turned on the radio to listen to the news and President Truman's address but after a few minutes tuned in a station that played local bands and singers hoping to be the next Jo Stafford. She looked at Tom sitting in the armchair across from hers, the one that used to be John's.

She and her husband had only lived as newlyweds for four months before the war began and he went to serve, but in that time she had many memories of him in that chair. Tom looked foreign and completely wrong there, and wearing John's old clothes.

He stood and walked to the mantle to examine the photographs. He touched the gilt frame of their wedding photo. "Your husband?"

"Yes, that's John. He made it through almost four years of war and was wounded just before the end. He died in a hospital overseas."

Tom moved on to another photograph. "These are his parents?"

"Yes. He's the little boy in the picture, and that photo on the left is my parents. They live in Chicago."

She joined him at the fireplace, pointing to one picture after another. "That's my sister and me when we were thirteen and fifteen. These are my grandparents, my husband's grandparents, aunts, uncles, cousins."

She watched his face as he studied all of the photos. She longed to reach out and trace the blue swirl that followed his cheekbone. He blinked and the long, full brush of his eyelashes swept against that cheek. Beautiful.

He turned to her and she nearly backed away from the heat he radiated and those vibrant eyes piercing through her. "Family."

"Yes."

He ran his finger along the mantel top, looking thoughtfully at the pictures.

She wished there was something she could do to earn a smile from him, a real one that would show his teeth and fill his eyes with light. "Would you like me to read to you? Something funny, not the mermaid story."

Another of those half-smiles slightly curved his lips. "Yes."

She chose *Tom Sawyer* from the bookshelf and skipped to the chapter about Tom fooling his friends into whitewashing the fence for him and paying for the pleasure.

Tom sat on the floor, leaned against the armchair and watched her as she read. Every time Sarah glanced up from the story to check his reaction he was listening with intense concentration, but from beginning to end of the amusing tale he never once laughed or smiled.

In bed that night, Sarah could feel Tom's presence in the house. Rather than putting him in the loft, she'd allowed this strange man to sleep in the bedroom just down the hall from her. She was crazy. He might take her invitation to stay in the house as something more.

She'd fully intended to have him sleep in the barn but feared Reed might search outbuildings of local farms in the dead of night while the homeowners slept. It was safer for

Tom to be inside with her ... well, not *with* her but...

As she drifted toward sleep, visions of tattooed flesh floated through her mind. In the past twenty-four hours she'd seen more of Tom's body than she had of any man other than her husband. Now, as she drowsed, there was nothing to stop her from reaching out and touching his warm, colorful skin. In her fantasy he welcomed her touch. His eyes closed in pleasure as she ran her hands over his hard chest and down to his stomach. He groaned as her hands moved lower and she felt the length and girth of him, throbbing with heat and life.

Sarah moaned softly as her hand moved between her legs once more.

But when she slept at last she didn't dream of the tattooed man. Instead she had a vivid dream about John and the child they had never had. The three of them were on a picnic in the meadow where the carnival had been. Their golden-haired child was laughing under the summer sun.

She woke with a start, her heart aching for the loss of her husband and un-conceived child. She wept quietly into her pillow, pain covering her in a black cloud of sorrow.

Chapter Three

When Sarah woke the next morning, Tom was gone, or at least John's bedroom was empty. The covers were neatly pulled over the bed and her guest was not in the house.

She found him out in Edison's stall pouring feed into the box. He'd already pumped fresh water for the horse.

"Good morning," she said. "Thanks. You didn't have to do this."

"I want to help."

She stroked the white blaze on the horse's forehead. "Edison thanks you too. He gets tired of waiting for me in the morning."

Tom stood beside her and patted the old gelding's glossy neck. He looked down at Sarah and his eyes caught and held hers in another of those gazes that left her heart pounding. He didn't need to put his hands on her for her to feel she had been touched.

Once more she shook off the spell. "It's time for breakfast. When you're finished here, why don't you come on in the house?"

BONE DEEP

After the meal she asked Tom to clear the gutters and told him where to find the ladder in the barn. Meanwhile, she cleaned the house, made the beds and washed another small load of laundry, Tom's clothes only.

She considered simply throwing the rank things away. Before she dunked the grimy pants into the hot water, she checked the pockets. There was no change or keys, but jammed deep in the front pocket was a folded page torn from a magazine. Carefully she opened it and smoothed the well-worn creases of the limp paper.

It was an old advertisement for tourism in Virginia Beach. A happy family sat on a blanket, the parents sunning themselves and smiling fondly at their children building a sandcastle at the edge of the water. They were a picture-perfect family.

Sarah stared at the ad until her eyes blurred. She dashed away her tears and carefully re-folded the sad testament to an unlived life. She put it in her apron pocket then pushed Tom's pants into the steaming wash water.

Later when she called him in for lunch, she put the folded magazine page next to his plate.

He looked at it before sliding it into his shirt pocket without comment. He took a small bite of the ham sandwich Sarah had made for him. Obviously minding her etiquette lesson the previous day, Tom refrained from hunching over his plate and shoveling in food as he ate.

"How do you feel about splitting logs?" she asked after he'd finished. "It's not too early to get a stack ready for winter and I'm not the best chopper. I'd really appreciate the help."

He nodded, silent as always.

She showed him to the woodpile at the side of the house and demonstrated how to set the round logs on end and split them in halves, then quarters. She wasn't very good at it and her log toppled sideways with the ax still stuck in it.

Tom unbuttoned his shirt and slipped it off his shoulders. He wore no undershirt so his muscular biceps and chiseled chest were immediately on display. Sarah's stomach give a little flip as she quickly scanned his lean torso. It was hard not to stare at the fascinating designs and the body they covered.

He grasped the axe and un-wedged it from the log with a hard twist. He hefted the axe, brought it up over his head and down into the log with a solid thunk. His back and arm muscles flexed powerfully as he quickly split the log with a few well-placed blows.

Goosebumps raised on Sarah's arms and she rubbed them as she dragged her gaze away from the mesmerizing sight of a full-rigged ship on Tom's back tossing on waves of blue.

"All right. I'll leave you to it. I've got to change the oil on the Plymouth. I've been putting it off too long."

She could still hear the axe biting into the wood as she walked toward the driveway and she continued to picture what he looked like swinging that axe. Why couldn't she stop fantasizing about this man? Why was he getting under her skin? He barely spoke a word yet his presence was overpowering. She was aware of him all the time.

She growled at herself in annoyance and turned her

attention to the old sedan. She'd convinced Frank at the Texaco station to show her how to change the oil so she could do it herself and save money. She got the jack out of the trunk, placed it under the rear bumper and cranked until the car was raised off the ground. She crawled underneath the transmission bringing a pan with her to drain the oil into. The smell of oil and gasoline made her nose wrinkle.

She struggled to open the drain plug, cursing under her breath. Her wrench slipped on the plug and she grazed her knuckles on hard metal. With another curse, she reset the wrench and jerked on the stuck plug, afraid it would suddenly give way and she'd get a face full of oil. The plug refused to budge.

She put more muscle into it, grunting as she wrestled with the wrench. The car rocked a little with her exertion, but the wrench just slipped on the stubborn plug again.

"Damn it!" The edges of the plug were beginning to round off and she knew the wrench would only slip again. She pushed with all her strength, her wrists and shoulders straining in her cramped position beneath the car.

"Sarah!"

She heard her name and the sound of running feet. Hands grabbed her ankles and yanked her out from under the car. Tom dragged her roughly away from the vehicle.

Sarah's shirt rode up and her spine scraped over the gravel. As she started to protest, the heavy Plymouth slipped off the jack and hit the ground with a dull thud.

Sarah twisted around to see polished chrome and maroon paint only a foot away from her face. She scrambled up and crab-scuttled backward, away from the automobile that had been seconds away from crushing her. "Jesus, Mary and Joseph!"

Tom dropped to his knees behind her. "Are you all right?" His voice vibrated near her ear. She'd backed right into his arms and was pressed against his bare chest.

"Yes. I think so." She let out a shaky breath and looked at him over her shoulder. "You were clear on the side of the house. How did you know?"

"I saw it." His arms were wrapped around her, pressing against her breasts, fingers digging into her upper arms. His body was so hot against her back. "You were going to be hurt."

"What?" She shifted so she could see his face better. "How? What do you mean, 'you saw'?"

"Inside," he explained, looking down at her from several inches away. His eyes glittered like polished gems against the chaotic colors of his face.

"What does that mean?" But part of her already knew.

"I see things sometimes." He paused then added, "Like my mother did."

"The fortuneteller." A shiver ran through her; the elemental fear of the unknown and a reaction to the close call she'd just had.

In response to her trembling, he squeezed her even tighter against his sweat-slicked chest. His heart pounded beneath her ear. He stopped digging his fingers into her arms and began to caress them instead. Hot licks of fire rocketed straight down to her crotch. Her nipples peaked in such sharp response, she feared he'd feel them pressing into his arm even though her blouse and bra.

His hands smoothed up and down her arms, and his face hovered above hers, eyes trained on her mouth as he leaned closer.

A soft exhalation escaped her. Her face tilted up. Then the realization of what was about to happen hit her. She twisted out of his grasp. "You can let go now. I'm okay."

He dropped his arms from her as if he'd been scorched.

As she scooted away, a pang went through her at the loss of those sheltering arms around her. She touched her lips with her fingertips and glanced at Tom.

He knelt, hands clenched into loose fists against his thighs. His chest moved in shallow breaths and his gaze slid away from hers to stare at the ground.

For a moment they remained frozen several yards apart.

Sarah broke the silence. "So your mother had real psychic powers."

He sat back on his heels. "Sometimes."

She brushed the embedded gravel from her palms. "And you have flashes sometimes, like the dream you mentioned. You told me yesterday you'd seen me before in a dream."

He nodded once.

She pushed herself up to her knees. "What happened in that dream?"

He shook his head, still studying the ground. "Nothing."

Sarah was curious about the dream, but dropped the subject.

"How often do you have these premonitions, and how often do they come true?" She was excited yet dismayed by the idea of someone possessing such powers. She'd been raised in a Christian and even though she hadn't attended church or talked to God much since John's funeral, old beliefs died hard. The minister would've said it was against nature and maybe even a sign of the devil to be able to see the future.

Tom looked at his hands, clenching and unclenching them slowly. "When people come to look at me, sometimes I see pieces of their lives. I don't know if it's something that's going to happen or something already past. It's just ... pictures."

"But you knew today that the car was going to fall on me."

"Yes." He looked into her eyes again. "You were going to be hurt. I couldn't let that happen."

She exhaled, trying to comprehend everything he'd told her. It seemed outlandish, but the proof was in the solid Plymouth sitting barely a yard away from her with the jack lying on its side beneath it.

"Thank you. You probably just saved my life."

Tom smiled at her then, the tiniest lift of the corners of his mouth, eyes crinkling a little.

Suddenly Sarah laughed giddily, overcome by the intensity of her brush with danger. "I just realized. I still have to change the stupid oil."

He rose to his feet. "I can do it for you."

"No. I need to get back on the horse," she said, standing up too.

He looked at her blankly.

"It's an expression. It means facing your fears."

He nodded.

Tom helped her place the jack and make sure the Plymouth was securely seated on it this time. When Sarah continued to struggle with the wrench, he took over in typical male fashion, turning the plug with infuriating ease. He placed the pan beneath the drain and climbed out from under the car.

"I'll finish up," she insisted. "I need to be able to do this myself."

Still he stood by while the oil drained into the pan and checked to make sure the drain plug was secure after Sarah had screwed it tight.

"Men," she mumbled, picking up the container of oil and carrying it to the refuse pit to dispose of it.

When she returned, Tom had let the car off the jack and was opening the hood to add oil.

"I told you, I can do it." Sarah's tone was sharper than she intended, and she felt awful when he stepped quickly away from the engine. "Sorry, I didn't mean to snap, but, a woman living on her own needs to be able to take care of things like this. But if you want to chop some more firewood, I wouldn't stop you."

Obediently he started toward the back yard.

"Tom, wait." She walked over to him and took his hand, smiling up at him. "Thank you again for saving me."

He nodded and his eyes creased at the corners again.

She found she didn't want to let go of his hand, but forced herself to step away after a moment. He looked at her for another second then turned and headed around the corner of the house.

Sarah filled the engine with fresh oil, wiped her hands and slammed the hood shut. Checking her watch, she saw it was already time to begin preparing dinner if she was going to have the pot roast ready by six o'clock.

While she washed vegetables at the kitchen sink, she watched Tom through the window, chopping wood. He was such an odd man, unlike anyone she'd ever met. While much of that probably had to do with his strange upbringing, she felt there was more to it than that. There was a far-seeing look in his eyes that made her think of angels, or mythological stories of gods who walked among men.

She wished she could get him to talk more. Their meals together had been mostly silent and she'd been forced to carry on one-sided conversations. She wanted to know more about him, how much he understood about the world, or if he had been imprisoned in ignorance. It would be a slow process to draw him out.

Sarah suddenly realized that in one day she had decided to let him remain here. Without discussing it or asking him his plans, Sarah knew that he was here to stay. Taking on the responsibility of hosting him was overwhelming, but also a comfort. The farm hadn't felt so much like 'home' in a long time. The desolation she'd experienced since John's death had receded a little and for the first time in months, she felt an interest in something. Maybe too much interest.

Outside the kitchen window, Tom's muscular arms emblazoned with bold colors lifted the axe and brought it down in methodical strokes. Sarah watched his smooth movements and rippling back muscles and once more that trapped-bird flutter inside her started up.

She focused on the potato she'd pared to almost nothing and kept her gaze firmly away from the window.

After supper that night Sarah and Tom retired once more to the living room. She built a small fire to ward off the chill and they sat before the fireplace in the two armchairs. Again Sarah listened to the news on the radio, but she noticed Tom looking at the *Tom Sawyer* book on the shelf like an anxious dog waiting for its food bowl to be filled. Why couldn't he just tell her what he wanted?

She realized if she waited for him to say something, she'd be waiting until dawn so she finally asked, "Would you like to hear more of the story?"

"Yes."

Tom had said he could read a little. She'd like to find out how much. "Why don't you follow along with me in the book? We'll look at the book together."

They stretched on their stomachs on the rug in front of the crackling fire, arms propped on throw pillows from the couch. She opened the book to the first chapter this time and began to read.

"'TOM!' No answer. 'What's gone with that boy, I wonder? You TOM! No answer. The old lady pulled her spectacles down and looked over them about the room; then she put them up and looked out under them."

Sarah ran her finger along under each word, pointing out the places where Tom's own name was printed. When she glanced sideways, he was frowning at the black print and her moving finger.

They were shoulder to shoulder. She felt heat radiating from his body and the warm skin of his arm brushing against hers. Her attention was distracted from the story as she stole a look at the tattoo on the back of his hand stretched out beside hers. A bright sun had flaming rays which licked out from the solar disc up his fingers and around the sides of his hand toward his palm.

Sarah brought her attention back to the book and read quickly through the abridged version. Some of the language was quite old fashioned and she didn't want to lose Tom's interest. Soon she reached the passage in which Tom met Becky Thatcher.

"He worshipped this new angel with furtive eye, till he saw that she had discovered him; then he pretended he did not know she was present, and began to show off in all sorts of absurd boyish ways, in order to win her admiration."

She stopped. "Tom, do you want to try to read a little bit."

He shook his head and tapped the page for her to go on.

Sarah continued until she reached the description of Huck Finn.

"Huckleberry came and went, at his own free will. He slept on doorsteps in fine weather and in empty hogsheads in wet; he did not have to go to school or to church, or call any

being master or obey anybody."

She was struck by the similarity to Tom, a rootless man with no place to call home. She was glad she hadn't chosen to read Huckleberry Finn with its harsh descriptions of the boy's abuse by his father, far too similar to Tom's real life. However, Huck had escaped to freedom so maybe it was a story that Tom would enjoy.

He nudged the back of her hand, letting her know she'd paused too long. "Go on."

She smiled but closed the book. "My throat's sore. I can't read any more." She turned toward him and his face was right in front of hers. "Tom, growing up in that place was there anyone who you talked with? Anyone who was a friend? All those years--there must have been someone."

He traced the illustration on the cover with his finger. "Bernard. He talked to me sometimes, brought me things to eat. He's the small man you saw."

"The midget? Where do all of those people come from? All the people in the"—she almost said 'freak show' but changed it to—"sideshow?"

"Everywhere. People who belong there find their way."

Sarah thought that no one belonged in such a bizarre, nomadic world.

He turned on his side to face her and propped his head on his hand. "Tell me about your family." It was the first time he'd made a direct request.

He was so near she could see the shadow of stubble growing on his scalp, blurring the images there. She felt self-conscious talking with his eyes riveted on her.

"Well, I'm from Chicago originally. I met John when we were in college. He was in the agricultural program. We got married and moved here to Fairfield after his father died and left him the farm. His mother had passed away some time before. Now that John is gone I don't know what keeps me here. My parents want me to come home to Chicago but ... I'm not ready to leave here."

Sarah was afraid to find out that she was just as lonely in Chicago as she'd been on the farm. Maybe there was nowhere on earth where she wouldn't be lonely without John.

"My husband enlisted soon after we moved here. We never really got a chance to make this place our home together, and now it's too late."

Sarah sat and crossed her legs, holding the throw pillow on her lap. "My sister is married and lives in California so I haven't seen her in years. I really miss her. We fought like cats growing up, but we were close too. Letters and phone calls aren't the same as spending time together."

As he listened, Tom rotated his left shoulder and winced.

"You did a lot of chopping today. If you're not used to it, you'll probably be really sore by tomorrow. You need some liniment on your muscles."

Sarah got up and went to the bathroom for the ointment. She stopped to look at herself in the mirror, her gaze locked with her own hazel eyes. "What are you doing?" She was about to give a man she barely knew a massage and couldn't deny it was partly because she wanted to touch him so badly.

Back in the living room, Tom sat cross-legged, gazing into the fire. She knelt behind him, sitting on her heels.

"You'll need to take off your shirt." Her cheeks burned although she tried to sound clinical.

He obeyed as Sarah unscrewed the cap and squirted a dollop of liniment on her palm. The ointment heated between her palms and the strong smell of mint and camphor rose. She placed her hands on Tom's shoulders and began to massage the taut muscles. He faced the fire and held very still as she touched him. Tension coiled in the muscles under his warm skin. She kneaded from his neck across the top of his shoulders, trying to pull the tightness out.

He inhaled sharply as she dug into the tender muscles.

"Am I pressing too hard? John always complained I hurt more than I helped."

"No." His voice was barely above a whisper. "It's good."

The sensation of his hot skin beneath her hands sent waves of desire through her, rolling like the ship tossed on the waves of his back. Her sex ached and she clamped her thighs together, trying to ignore her growing lust.

As she kneaded his back, she was able to examine his body art at close range at last. Above the large ship between his shoulder blades was a starry sky. In the water below were fishes, mermaids and sea monsters. On his lower back, beneath the ocean floor, the flames of hell crackled and demons danced. The scene was interrupted by the waistband of his trousers--John's trousers. She wanted to see what happened below but her view stopped at his waist and her hands did too.

She thought about John and how he would admire that beautiful sailing ship, so like one of his models. Then she thought about the hours of pricking needles that such a complex tapestry had required. It must have been painful and unrelenting. She brushed her hand over the beautiful, awful design once more then started on his arms.

From his bulging biceps she worked down to his forearms where the angel and the devil dwelled. His muscles were so hard and his flesh so warm beneath her stroking hands. She had to lean close in order to reach all the way down to his hands, and the heat of his back baked into her. She inhaled his scent, soapy and clean but with an undeniable musk of maleness underneath.

By the time she'd finished the massage, her hands ached from kneading and pressing. She ran them lightly over the silky skin of his back once more then clasped his shoulders. "Done."

It occurred to her that beyond an occasional moan when she hit a sensitive spot, Tom had remained silent throughout the massage. More than silent, completely still. His head was bowed and he trembled slightly.

"Tom, are you all right?" She rested her hand between his shoulders and leaned around to peer into his face.

He looked at her with anguished eyes. Tears instantly sprang to her eyes in response, and she murmured, "I'm sorry," even though she didn't know what she was apologizing for. She gently rubbed the back of his neck.

He closed his eyes and a tear escaped to trickle down his cheek.

"Sh, it's all right," she soothed, continuing to stroke his neck. If his story was true, he'd probably not been touched by gentle hands since he was very young. Her heart ached at the thought of so many years of loneliness and isolation. She'd suffered a bit of that with the loss of her husband, and could imagine that pain magnified a hundredfold, with absolutely no one caring for his welfare.

She slid her arms around Tom and gathered him close. She rubbed his back and cradled his shorn head. His face nestled into the crook of her neck. After a moment, his arms slid around her, crushing her against him.

"Sh," she continued to murmur as she rocked back and forth. It felt so good to be in a man's arms again and she was taking comfort as much as giving it. She held him until his trembling subsided and for many long, silent moments after that.

Her cheek pressed against his head, the stubble growing on his scalp scraping her cheek, and the heat between them began to build. His hands glided over her back then moved up to slide into her hair.

His face shifted in the hollow between her shoulder and neck, and she realized with a start that he was inhaling her scent and brushing his lips lightly over her skin. She held her breath as the sensation in her private parts grew from a dull ache to sharp need. She closed her eyes and almost moaned her pleasure at his breath brushing the hollow above her collarbone.

But, oh God, this wasn't right. She mustn't. She was in mourning and Tom was too different, too damaged, too strange. She pulled away from him.

He stared into her eyes, freezing her like a wild animal in bright headlights. Their faces were only inches apart. His startlingly pink tongue swept out to lick his lips. Her own mouth opened in response. It would be so easy. A slight inclination of her head and their lips would touch. She felt his warm breath and started to lean in, forgetting all the reasons she shouldn't.

Just then a log snapped loudly in the fireplace, sending out a shower of sparks.

They both turned toward the fire, the intense mood broken. She got up, grabbed the poker and extinguished the live embers that were burning tiny holes in the hearthrug. Then she hung the poker on the rack and shut the doors on the dying blaze.

"It's been a long day. I think I'll go to bed now."

She didn't look at Tom as she spoke. She knew she had to get some distance from him or something would happen that couldn't be undone.

Tom rose too and stood before the fire watching her extinguish the lights around the room. When she'd was finished, they stood in the dim living room, making no move to go upstairs.

And then his husky voice floated through the darkness. "Thank you."

"You're welcome." She understood that he was thanking her for more than a massage and wished she could offer him even more comfort, more sympathy, but it wasn't possible.

She led the way upstairs and bid Tom good night in the hallway. It was a relief to close her bedroom door behind her. She leaned against it for a moment, feeling as if she'd just escaped intentionally diving over the edge of a cliff.

After preparing herself for the night, she sat in bed reading a magazine article about Truman's vision for post-war America. But after a half hour of reading the same paragraph, she gave up and tossed the magazine aside. Staring out the window at the night sky, she wondered what she'd gotten herself into by inviting Tom into her home. What was she allowing to develop between them? It was wrong, but God it had felt so good holding him and being held. With a groan of frustration, she grabbed the pillow, and hugged it tight.

It was going to be another restless night.

Chapter Four

The next morning as Sarah fried potatoes and eggs for breakfast, she had to admit it was a pleasure not to have to rush to take care of the animals first thing. Tom had taken on that chore. And it was a pleasure to be cooking for two again. It gave her a warm feeling knowing he'd walk in the back door any minute with a steaming pail of milk, and then sit down at the table to eat what she'd prepared for him.

But none of that made it any easier to meet Tom's eyes following the intimate moment they'd shared the previous night. The silence over breakfast felt awkward and uncomfortable and Sarah finally interrupted it with a brisk announcement.

"I'm going to go into town this morning. I have errands to run. Will you be all right here on your own?"

He nodded.

Before leaving, Sarah assigned Tom the task of cleaning Edison's tack and asked if he'd scrape the picket fence, preparing it for a coat of paint. Once again she realized they weren't discussing when he'd be moving on. It was almost a given that he was going to stay.

BONE DEEP

A last look in her rearview mirror as she drove away showed Tom growing smaller behind her. He lifted a hand and Sarah waved back with an odd feeling of loss, as if he might not be there when she returned.

At the general store, Mrs. Davidson enthusiastically greeted her. Her husband owned the shop, but his formidable wife ran it ... and the Ladies Auxiliary at the Methodist Church, and the church choir, and the quilting club, and the annual bake sale and bazaar. She ruled the social world of most of the ladies in Fairfield.

"Sarah, I'm so glad to see you. I've been worried. I told Dan to send that worthless Harold to check on you since the boy had deliveries to make out your way, but Dan forgot to tell him. You should think about installing a phone, dear."

Sarah picked up a shopping basket. "I'm fine. Why were you worried?"

"Didn't that carnival man Reed stop by your house and tell you about the escaped loony? I thought he'd been to every farm around." Mrs. Davidson spoke while putting a new paper roll in the cash register. "It's terrifying is what it is, like having a wild animal or crazy person from the mental hospital running loose. Anything could happen. And there you are, all alone out on that farm. It's not safe."

The shopkeeper beckoned Sarah closer, leaning over the candy display to whisper. "People are saying this freak once hurt a girl who went to the carnival. They say she was assaulted." She raised her eyebrows to make sure Sarah understood the sexual connotation of the word. "You be sure and lock all the doors and windows at night. You should get yourself a watchdog."

"I'll think about it." Sarah started down the dry goods aisle of the store.

Mrs. Davidson came out from behind the counter and followed her, her double chin bobbing as she rattled on. "That Reed fellow left town late yesterday. But the law is on the hunt now. The carnival man said he didn't want the sheriff's office involved, but that's crazy. It's all of us who are in danger from this freak."

Sarah plucked a can of mushrooms from a shelf. "I don't know, Mrs. Davidson, from what Reed said the man's not a danger to anyone."

"Well, of course he'd *say* that, but any man who'd mark himself up like a savage can't be right in the head." She realigned the canned mushrooms to fill the gap Sarah had made. "Who knows what perverted things he's capable of."

With a non-committal "Hm" Sarah chose several cans of fruit. "So the police are involved now?"

Mrs. Davidson followed her up the aisle, straightening behind her. "Anybody who sees anything unusual, signs of somebody staying in their outbuildings, clothes missing off the line or vegetables from their gardens, is supposed to call the sheriff's office."

"I'll keep that in mind." Sarah moved from the row of canned goods to the store's limited produce display and picked a few oranges and bananas.

"I'm telling you, you need yourself a good guard dog living out there alone. Jenny Samuels' bitch had a litter. You should stop by and talk to her."

Sarah was doubtful that a little puppy could frighten away anything, but it was usually easier to simply agree with Mrs. Davidson's chatter. "I'll think about it."

The shopkeeper continued to proclaim her opinions while Sarah gathered the rest of her groceries and brought them up to the counter.

As she rang up the purchases, Mrs. Davidson offered one more piece of advice. "I heard through the grapevine you went to the carnival with Andrew Hooper. He's a good, solid, respectable man. You could do worse."

Sarah blinked. The grapevine could strangle you in this tiny town where nothing stayed private for long. "Yes, well..."

She held out her hand to accept her change. Mrs. Davidson made her wait for it while she expounded.

"You know, dear, you're not the only one who's lost someone. You mustn't grieve forever. It's our patriotic duty as women and Americans to take up the pieces of our shattered lives and start anew. Andrew Hooper would do very nicely for you."

Sarah's mouth stretched in a frozen smile. Her hand was still extended, but Mrs. Davidson held her change tantalizingly out of reach. Sarah thought it might be worth the extra time and gas to drive over to Hooperstown to shop from now on.

"Well, that's all I'm going to say, but it was about time somebody spoke to you about these things."

The busybody slowly counted change into Sarah's hand. She put the change in her purse, grabbed her bags of groceries and headed for the door.

"Think about what I said," Mrs. Davidson called out before the door closed behind Sarah.

Her next stop was the library. She selected a book on plumbing, a couple of mystery novels for herself and an illustrated book of King Arthur tales for Tom. She wanted to check out some beginning readers for him, but there was no way she could without stirring the librarian's curiosity. It would seem odd enough to Agnes that Sarah was suddenly interested in a child's book of Arthurian legends. Lack of privacy was one thing Sarah truly hated about living in a small town. She would certainly never dare to check out a racy novel for herself even if the tiny library possessed such a thing.

She carried her stack of books to the circulation desk where Agnes Chapman sat reading a newspaper. The white-haired librarian put down her paper and pushed her glasses up her nose. She accepted Sarah's library card and examined it as if she'd never seen it before, although Sarah came in at least once a month. The elderly woman was a queen ruling her small kingdom. Rule-breakers were unacceptable in her world and she accepted overdue fines with a disapproving air that made one feel like a petty criminal.

She handed Sarah her library card then stamped each book, stopping to check damage to the binding on the Round Table legends. She tsked mightily as she taped the spine.

Agnes pushed the stack of books across the counter. "I suppose you've heard about this circus person running loose."

BONE DEEP

Her nostrils flared in indignation. "These traveling carnivals shouldn't be allowed to exist. It's a wonder someone doesn't die on those ramshackle rides." She peered at Sarah. "Your house is right near where the carnival was set up, isn't it? You be sure and take extra care, young lady."

"Yes, ma'am." Everybody seemed far too concerned with her welfare today.

She put her books in the car and headed to McNulty's Hardware. It seemed everyone in town was gossiping about Tom. It shouldn't have surprised her. There wasn't a lot of excitement here. People would be remembering "the fall that crazy man escaped from the circus" for years to come, which didn't bode well for Tom.

Sarah had been too overwhelmed by the surprising advent of this stranger in her life to really think about the long term consequences. She couldn't hide him forever, and it didn't appear the townspeople would be receptive to letting him stay in the community. If anyone knew he was living in her house—that would be disastrous for her reputation.

She pushed open the door of the hardware store, ringing the bell over the door. Andrew Harper looked up from stocking a shelf and beamed at the sight of her.

"Sarah, hello!" He came over and half offered his hand to shake before dropping it to his side.

"Hi, Andrew. How's"—for the life of her she couldn't remember anything he'd told her about himself the other night— "the hardware business?"

"Busy. Everybody's getting things ready for winter. I've sold a lot of caulk and weather stripping."

57

"That's good." She looked past him toward the paint aisle as awkward silence fell between them.

He cleared his throat. "Is there, uh, anything I can get for you?"

"Yes. I need a gallon of paint. Flat white while do. I'm repainting my picket fence."

"Oh, I see." He led her through the store. "Do you need any brushes or turpentine?"

"Some turpentine, I guess."

They walked to the paint aisle. "Have you heard the news about that tattooed man?"

She picked a brush from one of the hooks in the pegboard. "Yes."

Andrew hefted a gallon of paint and a can of turpentine off the shelf and carried them to the checkout counter where he rang them up. "It's so strange to think we actually saw him up close and now he's God knows where. Kind of sad, though, isn't it? I mean, it sounds like the guy's lost more than anything. Like a little kid. We should probably have search parties out looking for him or something."

"I guess so." Sarah paid for the supplies and started to lift the box.

"Let me get that for you." Andrew hurried around the counter. He carried the box out to her car and stowed it in the trunk between bags of groceries. He closed the lid and turned to lean against the car.

"I had a real nice time the other night." He folded his arms and scuffed his shoe on the pavement. "I wondered if you might like to go out again some time ... with me. There's a dance over in Chadwick on Friday. Grace and Mike are going. Maybe we could double again."

"Oh! I don't know. I might be..."

He must know her schedule wasn't busy. She was a widow living alone on a farm. Her social life wasn't exactly buzzing.

"I'll have to think about it." She didn't want to have to find a polite way to say no. She didn't want to have to make excuses to Andrew Harper at all.

"Oh, sure." He ran a hand through his crew cut and rubbed the back of his neck. "Maybe I could stop by later in the week to find out what your answer is. I mean, since you don't have a phone. And if you need help painting that fence, I could do that for you."

She didn't want to deal with him a second time, especially not at her house with Tom hiding somewhere like a rainbow-colored ghost. Sarah took a deep breath.

"Andrew, I think you're a swell guy. Really. But I'm not ready to start dating anybody yet. I don't know what Grace told you, but I'm just not."

"I understand." Andrew nodded, frowning and flustered. "I didn't mean to be pushy. I know you must still be grieving, but, just so's you know, if you ever are ready to date again, I'd sure like to take you out."

"Thank you." Sarah managed a smile and moved around the car toward the driver's side. "I'm sorry, Andrew. Maybe sometime."

He rushed to open the car door for her. "That'd be great. I'm sorry I asked so soon. I didn't mean to upset you."

"I'm not upset. It's okay." She slid behind the wheel and started the engine, anxious to get away.

Andrew closed the door and stepped back.

Sarah pulled away from the curb. When she looked into her rearview mirror, Andrew was still standing there watching her drive away—another figure receding into the distance behind her. She thought she would cheerfully kill Grace May right now for creating this situation. Andrew was a sweet, friendly man and she hated bursting his hopeful expectations.

Driving home, Sarah was almost to the turn off for the farm when saw the sheriff's cruiser approaching from the opposite direction. The red light on top flashed and the siren gave a brief whoop.

Sarah stopped in the middle of the road parallel with the other car. Heart pounding she cranked down her window.

Deputy Phil Olkowski lowered his window. "Hi there, Mrs. Cassidy. How are you doing?" The deputy removed his cap and ran a hand over his forehead. His face was red and sweating. He blew out a long breath. "It's shaping up to be a hot one for September."

"Yes, it is." Sarah's pulse raced as if she'd been caught in a crime. "What's going on? I heard about this missing man from the carnival."

"Yeah, some poor, benighted idiot wandered off, but to hear folk talk you'd think a murderer was on the loose." He shook his head and put his hat back on. "Anyway, I was out to your place to see if you'd noticed anything unusual. Your farm is about the closest to where they was camped, except for

Charlie Burkett's. I hope you don't mind but I took the liberty to poke around your barn and outbuildings. Didn't see anything out of order though. I think you're safe."

"Well, thank you for checking, Phil. I feel safer knowing you're on the job." Sarah's heart slowed down. "If I spot anything unusual, I'll let you know."

"You can call me from the Burkett's. You know, you should get yourself a phone installed. They've already run a line to Burkett's. Yours isn't much farther. It's not safe for a woman living alone with no way to call for help."

"I've been thinking about it. I'll look into it." She smiled and started to roll up her window to end to the conversation.

"If you do happen to see this retarded fellow, no matter how harmless he seems, you go get Charlie or else call me and I'll come out. Better safe than sorry."

"I will." Sarah resisted the urge to gun the engine as she drove away. She turned onto her road and a half-mile later into her driveway. Climbing out of the car, she noticed a section of the picket fence around the house was scraped smooth for painting.

"Tom," she called, and for one heart-breaking moment, she was certain he wouldn't answer. Of course, he'd left when the deputy came around. Her brief adventure and budding friendship was over.

Then Tom emerged from the barn and walked toward her.

Relief and joy surged through her. Funny how quickly his strange face had become familiar and dear to her. She met him halfway across the yard.

"Are you all right? I talked to the deputy and he said he'd been by. I guess Reed left town. Maybe he didn't want the police hunting for you, but everyone in Fairfield does. Are you sure I can't take you to the sheriff's office so we can explain everything and straighten this out? You haven't done anything wrong. It's not as if they can arrest you."

He frowned. "No! If you want me to leave, I'll go, but not to the police."

"Why? You can explain your side of the story."

"They'll want me to go back." The deep furrow in his brow twisted the swirling tattoos on his forehead into new shapes. His jaw set stubbornly. "Anyone can see I belong with the carnival and that's where they'll take me."

"They wouldn't try to return you to Reed, not after I tell them how he's abused you. They'll see you're not dangerous, that you're normal."

"I'm *not* normal." For the first time since she'd met him, his voice raised. He glared at her and spread his hands, indicating his body. "Look at me."

She did as he bid, trying to see him as others would-- strange, freakish, different. But all she could see was Tom, and he looked beautiful to her.

"All right. Whatever you want. I'm not asking you to leave." She smiled reassuringly as she soothed him, then added lightly, "Besides, if you left, who would finish the fence for me?"

Still frowning, he looked at the portion of wood he'd scraped. "I'm sorry I didn't finish it."

BONE DEEP

She laughed and nudged his arm. "I'm kidding! You have to learn when people are teasing. Here's what we'll do. If you'll help me put away the groceries, we'll have lunch then scrape the rest of the fence and put on the first coat of paint. After that we can go to the pond and swim because I think it's going to be a scorcher this afternoon."

He looked up at the clear blue sky. "A storm will come through tonight and cool it off again."

Sarah raised an eyebrow. "Did you have a vision?"

"No. The air feels thick and heavy. It will break later."

"Good. We could use some rain."

Together they unloaded the car then Sarah made sandwiches and soup. Tom devoured his food with his usual gusto. She was pleased by his enjoyment of anything she set in front of him no matter how simple the fare. Then she remembered why he was so eager about food and her pleasure vanished.

Scraping peeling strips of paint from the fence took longer than expected. Sarah broiled under the hot sun. Her sleeveless blouse clung to her back and was soaked underneath her arms. She wiped sweat off her forehead and glanced over at Tom.

He was just as sweaty as she, but it looked better on him. Once more he'd removed his shirt--he seemed to have no discomfort with being half-undressed much of the time--and his colors shone under the blazing sun. She wondered if the pigments protected him from sunburn.

At last Sarah stood, stretched her aching lower back

and grimacing at the gallon of paint sitting in the grass. "You know what? Let's save the painting until tomorrow morning when it's cooler. I think we've earned a swim."

She provided Tom with John's old swim trunks then dressed in her own modest one-piece suit with a blouse and shorts over it. Her inner voice warned her it was a bad idea to go swimming with Tom, both of them nearly naked together, but she ignored the voice. It was a hot day and they could surely paddle around in the water for an hour without attraction getting the better of them.

They trekked across the fallow field toward the pond at the edge of Burkett's woods. Weeds scratched Sarah's bare legs. Blackbirds flew up from the tall grass at their approach and chirping crickets went suddenly silent.

Sarah could smell the pond before they reached it. The east side was mostly swamp water and cattails and the smell of algae and mud was pungent. But the rest of the pond was clear enough. They stopped on the muddy bank to remove their clothes.

"The local kids come out here sometimes, but we should be safe today. They wouldn't be home from school yet."

She unbuttoned her blouse and took it off. Even though she was still fully clothed in a bathing suit when she was finished, the act of removing it in front of Tom felt somehow sinful. Sliding her shorts down her hips, she refused to glance over and see if he was watching her.

Still without looking his way, she dove into the water. It was a little tepid and muddy but refreshingly cool compared to the steamy air. She swam to the opposite side where the cattails grew and halfway back again before she finally looked at Tom.

He stood on the muddy bank, testing the water with one foot. John's navy swim trunks covered him from his waist to mid-thigh and in that moment, Sarah would have given anything to have them disappear so she could see all of him.

"Can you swim?" she called.

He looked at her with a small smile and dove in, cutting cleanly through the water, resurfacing then stroking toward her. He looked like a glistening wet jigsaw puzzle, his colors pure and rich in the reflecting light. He swam slowly around her.

Sarah trod water, waving her arms beneath the surface to keep afloat. "This feels great. I was so hot." She leaned back and floated, eyes closed, aware of Tom still lazily circling her in a side-crawl.

His hand touched her heel lightly and she started, afraid for a moment he was going to duck her under. But he merely turned her in an easy circle, round and round like a floating leaf, as he swam.

Sarah relaxed and let him rotate her. With her eyes closed and body suspended, she felt weightless, almost bodiless. She realized he was playing with her, the first sign of anything remotely playful she'd seen from him, and she was touched.

After spinning her around for a while, he ducked underwater and swam away across the pond like a wild animal that had dared to come close then just as quickly retreated.

Sarah dove under the surface herself and shot off in pursuit of Tom. She caught up to him in the shallows, where her feet touched bottom and the water level stopped at her chest. Impulsively, she scooped water with both hands and drove it toward him.

He stood there letting it sweep over his head. He sputtered and blinked but didn't fight back.

"Come on. Race you across." She turned and swam toward the opposite shore.

In seconds he was beside her, and then ahead of her. He cut cleanly through the water while she churned in his wake. He stood in the shallows on the far side of the pond, waiting for her with a big smile on his face. His teeth were white against his brilliant skin and his eyes crinkled at the corners.

"So you're fast. How are you in a water fight?" She planted her feet on the muddy bottom and splashed him again.

When he continued to stand there, Sarah teased, "Show me what you got. Fight back."

He hesitated then pushed a wall of water at her.

Sarah retaliated. Soon the surface of the pond was a churning battleground. As she shrieked, choked and laughed, she realized Tom was laughing too--actually laughing out loud. She'd never heard such a beautiful sound as his deep-throated chuckle.

"Truce!" she finally called, holding up her hands. "Enough. I surrender."

He stopped immediately, but his smile lingered. Water beaded on his body and his long eyelashes. He was a beautiful sight and Sarah's heart beat faster just looking at him.

They waded out of the pond and stretched on the grass away from the muddy edge. Sun soaked into their bodies and Sarah closed her eyes, breathing in the scent of the pond, pine trees and the nearby wild grapes, sweet and overripe. The harsh chorus of cicadas in the trees lulled her to sleep.

She was awakened, disoriented, by Tom gently shaking her arm.

"You'll burn. We should go back." For a brief moment his hand lingered on her arm, trailing down her pale flesh toward her hand. "Your skin is pretty." His voice was low and admiring.

A tremor of lust shivered through her at his light caress. Drowsily she reached out her hand and stroked the angel on his forearm. "Yours is too."

He looked from her hand to her eyes, his gaze dark with desire.

Sarah was instantly awake. She snatched her hand from his arm as if she'd been burned, got up and began gathering her clothes. "You're right, we should go home now."

Again they trudged across the field. She wondered how long this tension between them could hold before it broke like the dark clouds rolling in on the horizon.

Just as Tom had predicted, there would be a storm before morning.

After bathing away the muddy pond water, Sarah cooked potatoes and pork chops for their dinner, while Tom prepared a salad under her instruction. They ate and once more retired to the living room and listened to the news followed by Harold Raimer's Music Hour.

Sarah had given Tom his library book to look through and he pored over the pages, examining each picture carefully as though trying to figure out the stories.

She closed her plumbing tutorial after she realized she wasn't going to be able to fix her pipe problem without a professional. "If you'd like, I could teach you how to read."

Tom looked up from his book and smiled. "Yes."

She could see the change in him from the tense man she'd met only a couple of days before. He was relaxed and completely at ease with her now.

"Let me get some things together and we can begin." She gathered paper and pencil, figuring she'd start with the basics of the alphabet unless he demonstrated that he was beyond that. She sat cross-legged on the floor next to him. Smoothing the paper against the hard surface of a book she drew a capital 'A' then glanced at him.

He lips parted as if he wanted to say something.

She smiled encouragingly. "What?"

"I already have one thing I can read. Bernard taught me the words." Tom reached in his pocket, took out the magazine page she'd found the day before and carefully unfolded it. Without looking at the words he recited, "Doesn't your family deserve the perfect holiday? Virginia Beach. Paradise at half the price. Virginia Tourism Board."

"That's good." Sarah's smile widened at his earnest recitation.

He stared at the picture. "I made up a story about the family."

She leaned forward, resting her arms on her knees. "Tell me."

Again he recited as though it was something he'd memorized well. "The family is on their holiday at the beach. The children play in the water and go out farther and farther. The brother gets washed away by a wave and his sister screams but the father runs into the water and saves him."

He smoothed the crease down the center of the page with one finger, stopping where it crossed the woman's face. "After their vacation the family goes back home. They have a house with lots of windows. Each of the children has a bedroom with a window that looks out at the sky and they each have a bed to sleep in and no one is allowed to come into their room to look at them or touch them. The father goes to work to make money to take care of the family and the mother cooks food. They eat three times a day and sometimes even more. When the children wake up in the morning they eat breakfast and go to school. They have a lot of friends and no one looks at them because they look just like everybody else. They go outside whenever they want and eat whenever they want. They have a dog too." He stopped abruptly and looked up from the picture to her face.

Sarah's throat was so tight she could hardly swallow. Tom had spoken more words telling the story of his dream life than he had in the past two days. He'd also hinted at more about the conditions of his captivity than she wanted to know. She cleared her throat. "Go on. It's a nice story."

He looked at the magazine page. "The father and mother touch each other but it's good. They lay together at night, and in the morning, when he has to go to work they kiss goodbye. Together they will make another baby for their family." He fell silent for a second then added, "That's all."

Sarah drew a deep breath and released it slowly, waiting for her voice to steady before she spoke. "It's a very good story. Are those the things you want for yourself?"

He began folding the advertisement. "But I can't have them," he said matter-of-factly.

"Why not?"

He shrugged as if it was obvious and she remembered his earlier declaration, *I'm not normal*. She had to admit it was hard to picture this strange man living a normal family life in an average community. His differences were stamped all over his body as well as hidden deep inside him.

Sarah chose her next words carefully. "So, Mr. Reed let people come to your room and ... touch you sometimes?"

"When they paid extra."

"Since you were young?"

"Yes." He returned the advertisement to his pocket.

Sarah was shocked. She had heard suggestions of such perversions, but her knowledge of sex outside of the marital bed was limited. Her mother had given her brief, vague instructions before her wedding night and John had taught her the rest of what she knew.

Tom picked up the pencil and neatly copied an 'A' beside hers. "When I had visitors I got extra food," he added casually.

Sarah felt sick. She didn't know what to say. "I'm sorry," she whispered.

He glanced up with a puzzled frown. "Why?"

Her eyes welled with tears and she fought them back. She would not help him by making him feel pathetic. "For what happened to you. For everything you had to live with." *And that I came to gape at you like everyone else, as though you were a sideshow attraction rather than a person.*

He offered the pencil to her. "Show me more."

Sarah understood. He was finished talking about his past. She tried to put the terrible things he'd told her out of her mind and turn her attention to teaching him the alphabet, but his words haunted her. *When they paid extra.*

She shuddered but took the pencil and wrote 'B,' both in uppercase and lowercase. By the end of an hour she was writing simple sentences like "The cat ate the rat" and Tom was reading them aloud. His mother must have long ago taught him the basics and he only needed a refresher to awaken that knowledge.

After their lesson, Sarah read another chapter of *Tom Sawyer*.

Outside the storm was getting closer. A rumble of distant thunder grew steadily louder. Flashes of lightning shone briefly through the window. At about ten thirty the storm finally broke. Thunder crashed almost overhead and gusts of wind billowed the curtains inward bringing damp fresh air into the room.

Sarah and Tom went around the house shutting windows, enclosing the house in stuffy humidity once more.

"Let's sit out on the front porch. It's too hot inside," she suggested. She poured them each a glass of lemonade and they sat on the porch swing, watching the wind-driven rain wash across the yard. The rain smelled cool and a misty spray dampened their faces even in the shelter of the porch.

The proximity of Tom sitting beside her made the hair on her arms prickle. She felt his presence, so vital and masculine and alive, in her very cells. Her body yearned for him. She longed to reach out for him and let nature guide them to what felt like an inevitable conclusion.

Being near him made her nervous, edgy, uncomfortable, yet at the same time, it seemed natural to sit with him in comfortable silence watching the storm. After about a half-hour the wind and rain slowly died down and drifted away.

"I think that's the end of the hot weather," Sarah said as the temperature perceptibly dropped with the passing of the storm. "Fall is here."

Tom swirled the ice in his empty glass and looked at the muddy yard. "The show will be traveling south for the winter soon."

"Reed won't be back looking for you again, will he?"

"I don't think so."

She put her hand on his arm and tingles vibrated through it. "You can stay here as long as you like."

He looked at her hand then into her face. His eyes were only deep shadows in the darkness, but Sarah knew how blue they were as he gazed intently at her.

"Thank you," he said.

"We should probably go in now." She rose and took his empty glass.

He followed her inside where they opened the windows to let fresh air back in the house.

Upstairs in the hall, they stood for a moment, facing one another, a sliver of time that seemed to stretch and pull as elastic as taffy.

With every fiber of her being Sarah wanted to take a step toward Tom, hold out her hand and invite him to her room.

"Good night," she said at last, heading into her bedroom and closing the door behind her.

She wasn't ready. She couldn't open her windows wide and let rain pour into her house, and she wasn't ready to invite this complicated stranger into her bed.

Chapter Five

Tom set his foot in the stirrup and swung his other leg over Edison's back, sliding into the saddle. He gathered the reins and looked at Sarah with a pleased smile.

She was perched on the corral fence shouting instructions. "Good. Now don't hold the reins too tight or too slack. Give him a tap with your heels and he'll start walking."

Tom nudged the horse, but Edison continued to stand and stare off into the distance.

"A little harder. He's old and lazy and doesn't want to move."

Tom obeyed and the bay horse wheezed wearily but plodded forward. He circled the corral twice slowly. Tom rode awkwardly but continued to grin. His delight was delightful to see.

"Good. Dig in your heels a little and he'll trot."

Tom followed her directions and Edison reluctantly increased his speed. Tom jounced up and down with each step.

"Let your legs take the impact. Brace your feet and rise up in the stirrups so you're not quite seated. Then you won't bounce."

He followed her directions and improved almost

immediately.

"Good job. You're a natural!"

After trotting around the corral a few times, Edison slowed then stopped completely, panting as though he'd run a racecourse instead of made a couple of circuits of the corral.

Sarah shifted her bottom on the hard board of the fence. "Keep him moving. You have to let him know you're in charge. Give him another kick and a slap with the reins."

Tom complied and Edison walked then trotted again. Rising smoothly up and down, Tom looked as if he'd been riding his whole life.

Sarah smiled at the pure enjoyment on his face. She knew he loved animals. He'd told her that one of his jobs in the carnival was to care for the livestock, but he'd never been allowed to ride. So she'd decided it was time to give Edison a workout.

Edison was a retired horse who served no function on the farm and didn't care to be ridden. Like the dog Sheba, he had been on the Cassidy farm much longer than Sarah had. He'd earned the right to enjoy the twilight of his life with a warm stall, plenty of food and no more physical exertion than was necessary to crop grass.

Now Tom encouraged Edison into a canter and it was clearly a strain for the old horse. After a brief burst of speed, he slowed and began plodding again, blowing out his breath and limping slightly.

Tom stopped, slid off the saddle and stooped to examine Edison's hoof.

Sarah jumped off the fence and walked over to them.

"Don't let him fool you. There's nothing wrong with him. He just doesn't like to be ridden."

Tom put the horse's foot down, straightened and moved in front of Edison to peer into his huge brown eyes. He petted the blaze on Edison's forehead and murmured something to the horse.

Sarah patted Edison's sweaty flank. "Good heavens, you'd think he'd run the Derby. Lazy old thing."

"He's tired." Tom moved around to the horse's side again and started unbuckling the saddle.

Sarah watched his efficient movements. "You ride well. Too bad there's not a real horse you can practice on."

Together they removed Edison's tack and rubbed him down before Tom led the animal to the pasture. The old horse rolled on his back in the grass to rid himself of the feel of the saddle.

"See, I told you he's all right. Look at him frisk around now."

They leaned against the split rail fence, watching Edison amble across the pasture without a limp while Millie the cow stood in the shade of a tree, occasionally pulling up a clump of grass.

Sarah smelled the horse scent on Tom mingled with his sweat and the essence of his body beneath that. It had been a strange week, living with him in her home. Time passed quickly, yet it seemed like he'd lived with her for much longer than a week. Every day she grew more used to having him around as their routine of chores, meals and evenings spent with music and books continued. She couldn't imagine her life going back to the way it was before Tom arrived, when her days stretched out before her in lonely bleakness.

She hadn't felt this alive since before the Army lieutenant arrived on her doorstep to tell her John had been killed in action. She had shut down on that day and not been able to rouse interest in anything or anyone until now.

But while she and Tom had developed an easy pattern, she was also prickly whenever they were together, as if wearing a mohair sweater against her skin. Deep inside she admitted that she'd never been this physically aroused by any man before--not even her husband.

Tom didn't talk much, but she didn't need him to. She knew he was there and listening to her. The mostly one-sided conversations didn't feel awkward as they had at the beginning. Occasionally he would interject a comment so she knew he was truly hearing her. And now that he was so much more relaxed he would sometimes come out with a dry observation that set her laughing. He was definitely not mentally deficient despite the bizarre circumstances of his life.

Now it was Friday again, a week since she'd first encountered Tom at the carnival. It was hard to reconcile that brief amount of time with the complete turnaround in her life.

She watched Tom watch the horse for a moment then tapped his arm. "You ready for some dinner?"

That night after supper they settled in the living room for another reading lesson when the sound of a car engine came from outside. Without a word, Tom closed the book and went upstairs.

Sarah went to the front hall and turned on the porch light. Looking through the glass she saw Mike and Grace's car. She stepped outside and closed the door behind her.

Grace and Mike got out of the car and Andrew Harper emerged from the back seat.

Sarah was taken aback at the sudden arrival of her friends but there was nothing she could do but smile in welcome. "Hello."

"Hi." Grace May walked toward the porch. "We came to get you to go to the dance in Camden at the Grange Hall."

"Oh, I don't know."

"Will Axtell and the Harmonizers are playing." Mike came up behind Grace and put an arm around her waist. "They're really good. I heard 'em last year in Hooperstown at the Cherry Festival."

"Come on, Sarah." Grace May lifted her eyebrows and rolled her eyes toward Andrew standing beside of the car looking uncomfortable. "We're not going to let you stay home on a Friday night. Go get dressed and come out with us."

"I..." Sarah glanced at Andrew. He smiled at her but dropped his gaze, seeming embarrassed that he'd ignored her express wishes about dating.

Grace started up the steps to the porch. "No arguments. Come on, I'll help you pick out something to wear."

"No!" Sarah stepped in front of the door. "I mean, no. I'll get changed. Why don't all of you sit out here on the porch? It's a beautiful night. I'll bring you something to drink while you wait."

Before Grace could argue, Sarah went inside. She

BONE DEEP

glanced at the stairs and thought of Tom waiting up in his room. She supposed it would be safe enough to invite her friends into the house but felt more comfortable with them out on the porch. If they heard the floorboards creak overhead, they might be suspicious.

In the kitchen, she took three bottles of Coca-Cola from the refrigerator, popped the tops and carried them out to the porch. Grace and Mike sat on the swing rocking gently while Andrew perched on the railing across from them.

"Sorry I don't have any beer," Sarah said, handing out the chilled bottles.

"Thanks." Andrew still looked embarrassed. He lowered his voice. "Look, I'm sorry to surprise you like this. Grace said—"

"It's okay," Sarah interrupted. "I'll be ready in a few minutes."

"Take your time. We're in no hurry," Grace said.

Back inside, Sarah raced upstairs and knocked at Tom's door. When he opened it, she was struck anew by his strangeness. Over the past days, she'd gotten so used to the way he looked that she hardly noticed his tattoos anymore.

"I'm sorry. It's my friends, the ones who were with me at the carnival last weekend. They want me to go out dancing and Grace won't take no for an answer."

He nodded.

"I feel bad leaving you here."

"It's all right. Go have fun." He smiled briefly then started to close the door.

Sarah hesitated, feeling guilty about leaving him alone.

"I shouldn't be back too late. Don't feel you have to stay in your room. Make yourself comfortable, listen to the radio or read. Get a snack from the kitchen."

He nodded again and closed the door softly.

Sarah went to her room and put on her dark green dress with the flared skirt, her dressy high heels and a little makeup. She brushed out her auburn hair, decided she didn't want to take the time to put it up and tied a green satin ribbon in it instead. With a last guilty glance at Tom's closed door, she ran down the stairs.

She sat on the porch for a while talking with her guests while they finished their drinks and wishing they'd hurry. She was painfully aware of Tom isolated in his room, hearing their voices and laughter drifting up through his open window.

"Did you hear that Frank's selling the Texaco station? I guess he and Maizie are moving south to be near their kids." Mike drew on his a cigarette and slowly puffed out a smoke ring.

Grace spoke over him, carrying on a parallel conversation as the pair of them often did. "Sarah, you won't believe what Trixie Ross did. She broke off her engagement with Steve!"

"Moving to Tallahassee, I guess," Mike continued.

"They've been going out since we were in high school. She's kept him on a string all this time and now she's dumped him."

"Too hot and too many alligators for me."

"I heard that she's taken up with some fellow from over in Camden. Maybe we'll see them tonight at the dance."

Grace set her empty Coke bottle on the porch rail beside the swing.

Mike checked his watch. "I guess we'd better be going or the dance'll be half over by the time we get there."

Grace stood. "We should get going." She frowned at Mike, who was sipping the last of his soda. "Hurry up and finish that or we'll be late."

Sliding into the back seat of the car next to Andrew, Sarah breathed in a cloud of his too-strong cologne.

He leaned over to whisper again, "Sorry about this. I didn't plan it. I know you told me you weren't ready to date, but Grace..."

"I know. When she makes up her mind, she doesn't stop until she gets her way." She laughed. "That's how she got Mike to pop the question when he was dragging his heels."

"So this isn't a date," Andrew said. "Just friends going to a dance and having a good time." He grinned and Sarah thought he looked like an overgrown schoolboy despite the flecks of gray at his temples.

"Okay." She smiled back.

They drove almost an hour to Camden. The parking lot of the Grange Hall was full. Music and lights poured out of the open doors of the brick building. Inside, the crush of bodies and mingled odors of sweat, cigarettes and various perfumes made it hard to breathe.

The dance floor was crowded. The band played *Sing, Sing, Sing*, which had the dancers swinging as best they could in the limited space. Mike was right, though The Harmonizers were no Benny Goodman Orchestra, they weren't half-bad.

Sarah found her head bobbing and her toe tapping to the beat.

"Let's try to find a place to sit," Grace yelled over the music.

They threaded their way through the crowd to the back of the hall without finding a single available chair.

"Hell, might as well dance then." Mike grabbed Grace by the hand and pulled her out onto the floor.

"Do you want to?" Andrew leaned down to ask Sarah.

She nodded.

A half-minute after they started dancing the song finished. The band slowed down the pace with the melodious *Moon Glow*. Sarah shuffled in a small circle in Andrew's arms and the dance floor grew more crowded as even non-dancers got dragged out to sway with their dates to the romantic tune.

Sarah was overpowered by Andrew's cologne at this close range. She tried to maintain a little distance between them but with the press of bodies she found herself rocking in a close embrace. His cotton shirt was hot and damp with sweat beneath her hand resting on his shoulder. His hand that clasped hers was also moist.

When the song was finally over, Sarah stepped back, fanning her face. "Whew, it's hot in here. Shall we find the others and step outside for a minute?"

"Sure. I'll get some punch too," Andrew agreed.

Soon the four of them were in the parking lot with cups of vodka-laced fruit punch. Clusters of people lingered near the door while couples took little walks into the woods or necked in steamy-windowed automobiles. It was peaceful outside after the clamor of music and loud voices within the building.

It didn't take more than two or three sips of the heavily spiked drink for Sarah's head to start swimming. She wasn't used to drinking these days.

She decided to fish for information about what the sheriff's office and people in general thought about the tattooed man now that a week had passed. "So, is there any news about this lost guy from the carnival?"

"No one's seen hide or hair of him," Grace said. "It's kind of strange since he isn't somebody you could miss seeing."

"Probably long since out of the area," Mike said.

"Or maybe the carnival owner found him again," Andrew suggested.

Sarah took a sip of her punch. "Sheriff's office still looking?"

"I guess so. Why? Are you nervous out on the farm?" Grace asked.

"No, just curious." Sarah quickly changed the subject, getting Grace fired up about Trixie Ross and the mystery man from Camden again.

After a breather, they returned to the dance. They jitterbugged and fox-trotted for several hours, lubricated by a lot of punch. By the time her friends dropped her off at home, Sarah was unsteady on her feet, not drunk, just happily tipsy.

Andrew escorted her to the front door with a hand on her arm. "I had a real nice time, Sarah. Hope we can do it again soon."

"It was fun." She smiled, but she didn't ask him to stop

by again. "G'night."

He dipped his head and pressed his lips to her cheek. "Good night." He turned and walked down the porch steps.

Sarah touched her hand to her cheek, surprised at his boldness after she'd told him she wasn't interested. But maybe he'd had a little too much vodka too.

She went inside, closed the door and leaned against it, squeezing her eyes shut then blinking them, trying to drive away the dizziness. Moving to the window beside the door, she watched until Mike and Grace's car drove away then called, "Tom."

There was no answer. Maybe he was already asleep.

She walked through the hall to the living room and sank down on the sofa with a sigh, kicking off her too-tight high heels and rubbing her ankle. She sat for several minutes, letting the blessed silence soothe her ears.

The front door opened then closed with a quiet click. For a moment her heart raced and she had visions of killers or that creepy Mr. Reed stalking down the hall.

"Tom?"

"Yes," he answered softly, coming into the living room.

"Hi. Where were you?"

"Out in the barn." He stood in the doorway.

She beckoned him over. "Come sit down. It hurts my neck looking at you over my shoulder."

He walked over and stood behind "his" armchair, resting an arm on the back. His eyes widened as he looked her over from head to toe.

She realized he hadn't seen her in anything but shabby housedresses or blouse and pants and she couldn't help but feel smug at the approval in his eyes. She knew the emerald dress made her auburn hair glow redder and enhanced her hazel eyes.

She stood up and twirled around once for him, her head spinning even after her body stopped moving. "Fancy, huh? I don't get much opportunity to dress up these days, but I was quite the fashion plate back in Chicago. Was your evening all right?"

"Yes." His gaze dropped from hers. "How was your dance?"

"Nice. Too crowded though."

Again she felt a stab of guilt for having fun with her friends while he was alone here with only the animals to keep him company. She walked over to the radio and switched it on. A swell of orchestral violins filled the living room with a smooth, seductive melody.

Sarah held out her hand to Tom. "Would you like to dance?"

Slowly he moved around the back of the chair and approached her with his arms down at his sides.

She placed his left hand on her waist and curved hers over his shoulder. She clasped his other hand. "Now, we move around a little. It's not hard. Hear the beat of the music, and move your feet with it."

Together they shuffled back and forth. Sarah felt the heat of his skin and the hard muscle and bone through his shirt. She breathed in the sweet smell of hay, the earthy musk of farm animals and beneath that his own male scent. Even though she stood in the same stance as she had with Andrew, this dance felt completely different.

She turned her head to the side and looked at their linked hands, her pale fingers wrapped around his colorful hand. She moved in closer, not quite resting her head on his chest, but willing to if he drew her nearer yet.

"Do you like that man?" he asked, his voice a quiet rumble.

"What?" She looked up into his eyes, so dark they were almost navy rather than their usual crystal blue.

"That man who kissed you. I saw from the barn."

"Andrew? Oh no! He's just a friend. Yes, I like him but not in that way." Sarah felt she was back in grade school. *Do you like him? Or do you* like *him like him?*

"It was only a friendly kiss," she explained.

"Am I your friend?" His voice was low and sent a shiver up her spine.

Her tongue darted out to touch her lips. "Yes." The word came out a whisper.

"Can I kiss you?"

She caught her breath. A dozen logical reasons to say 'no' clamored in her mind, beating at the door of her consciousness to be let in. If she opened the door she would have to entertain each one like a bad houseguest. *He's too broken. You're too lonely. He's so different.* But she didn't want to hear from those logical thoughts tonight. She didn't want to invite them in, so she barricaded the door and exhaled, "Yes."

Tilting her face up, she closed her eyes and parted her lips in anticipation. After a moment's pause, she felt warm lips press quickly against her cheek like the brush of a moth's wings.

Sarah opened her eyes.

Tom stared down at her with his sapphire eyes.

That was all? It wasn't enough. Since she had already given herself permission to accept a kiss, she expected to get one. A real one.

She lifted her hand to stroke his cheek then gently guided his face toward hers. Tipping her head to the side so their noses wouldn't bump, she stood on her toes and pressed her lips firmly against his. A caress of his jaw and then she slid her hand around the back of his neck to pull him even closer.

He responded, his lips soft and pliant and opening for her teasing tongue which licked between them. Tom followed her lead, sweeping his tongue across her lips. His hand gripped her waist hard, pulling her tight against him. She felt the heat and hardness of his arousal even through jeans and taffeta.

He let go of her hand and cupped her face as he kissed her more deeply. Moaning quietly, he mashed his mouth feverishly against hers, desperate for deeper and deeper kisses.

His quiet moan and intense kisses spurred Sarah's desire. She moved her hand from his neck to his scalp, stroking the soft black fuzz that covered it now. She clutched his shirtfront to steady herself as the passionate kisses and too much vodka sent her head whirling and threatened her balance. At last she had to pull away to breathe.

She dropped down off her toes and gazed wide-eyed into his face.

Tom frowned and let go of her as if he'd been burned. "I'm sorry. I shouldn't have—"

"No, I want to. I just needed some air." She fanned her face with a hand. "There! Better now. Don't stop!" She grabbed his shirt with both hands and pulled him back to her.

His hands cautiously went around her waist once more then began moving up her back, feeling her body through the satiny fabric of her bodice. The full taffeta skirt was crushed between them. There was far too much material in the way, binding and hampering their efforts to get even closer. Need raged inside Sarah like a caged beast, roaring to be fed.

She broke off mid-kiss once more and reached behind herself to pull down the zipper of her dress. The bodice was a little tight and her ribs expanded when the zipper was open. She peeled off the dress, stepped out of the pool of green, and faced Tom again, clad only in her white slip and underwear.

He stared at her body then at her face. He reached out and touched her red-brown hair, smoothing the silky strands. "So bright."

"Irish," she explained. "My maiden name's O'Donnell."

He looked confused.

"Never mind." She stepped back into the circle of his arms, and there was no hesitation in his embrace this time. He gripped her tight and kissed her deeply, while violins on the radio filled the room with a sweet, soaring melody.

Sarah melted against his warmth, feeling soft, small and feminine in his strong arms. With her mouth still pressed to his, she backed him toward the couch. She laughed as he sat down abruptly, and she climbed onto his lap, straddling him. She felt giddy and light, free of the weight that had leavened her days during the past year and a half. Desire rushed through her. She wanted him without reservation or doubt, and she would have him.

Her slip was hiked up on her hips and her bare legs hugged his. The hard bulge in his pants rubbed against her crotch through her underwear and she ground against him, trying to relieve the dull ache. Sitting on his lap she was above him and he tilted his head back to gaze into her eyes. He looked stunned, as if he couldn't believe this was happening. His hands bracketed her waist and slid slowly up her sides toward her breasts, but halted short of actually touching them. His gaze dipped to her cleavage and Sarah could feel how much he ached to touch her.

She gathered the hem of her slip, pulled it over her head and cast it aside. His eyes riveted on the swell of her breasts over the lacy cups of her bra. He looked up with questioning eyes.

She smiled encouragingly. "Go ahead."

He stroked his fingers lightly over the top of each mound, treating her as if she were as delicate as porcelain.

Sarah reached behind herself and unfastened the hooks of her bra. She shrugged it down her shoulders and sent it sailing through the air to land beside her slip. She sat naked, but for her underpants, on the lap of a near stranger and had never felt so bold, so proud of her body, so unbelievably desirable and powerful in her entire life.

Tom's Adam's apple bobbed and he reached toward her chest. His right hand with the flame-colored sun and the left with its moon-and-stars motif closed around her full breasts and kneaded them gently. He rubbed the pads of his thumbs over her nipples. They tightened in response, sending a delicious twinge straight down to her sex and making her wiggle on his lap.

"Mm. That's nice," she whispered.

He glanced up at her and smiled so sweetly it hurt her heart. He continued to fondle her breasts carefully, toying with the nipples with intense fascination. Sarah didn't know how to tell him that it was all right to suck on them too. Finally she simply said it. "You can kiss them if you want."

She flushed at her brazen invitation. But it was obviously what Tom had been waiting for. He immediately leaned in and wrapped his lips around one aureole. His teeth grazed her nipple, his tongue lapped over it, and then he latched on and sucked.

She gasped at the sensation and cradled his head, urging him to continue with the pressure of her hand. His eyes were closed, long lashes fanning across prominent cheekbones. Tom's face was made up of severe lines: a straight, high-bridged nose, arched eyebrows, a sharp jaw and, balancing all that angularity, an almost feminine mouth with bowed upper lip and full lower one. Then there were those amazing blue eyes. With or without the manmade facial designs, he was a very striking man.

Sarah pushed Tom away from her breasts long enough to unbutton his shirt and pull it off his shoulders. When she started to lift his undershirt, Tom put his hands on hers. "Wait."

Lifting her off of his lap, he stood and crossed the room to turn off the lamp. Light from the hallway barely illuminated the room and cast deep shadows. Peeling off his undershirt, Tom returned to the couch and pulled Sarah back onto his lap.

She wanted to see him it seemed he didn't want to be seen. In some ways it felt even more intimate, cuddled together half naked in the semi-dark. She caressed his face with both hands then leaned in and placed a chaste kiss on his lips. Her hands slid down his neck and his warm chest, feeling his pulse beat rapidly under her palm. She continued on down his torso and over his taut belly, which twitched beneath her touch. She unfastened the button of his trousers and drew down the zipper.

Tom gave a sharp inhalation as she reached beneath the waistband of his underwear. His fully engorged cock filled her fist. It felt different from John's, and she realized he was circumcised. She wondered what that looked like and automatically turned her face down, though she could see nothing in the dark.

He grasped her chin and tipped her face up. "Don't." Light from the hallway illuminated his multi-hued arm as he touched her cheek. "Close your eyes and you can pretend it's your husband."

"What?"

"I know you miss him. I feel it coming off of you in waves all the time," he murmured. "Besides ... you don't want to see me."

She frowned. "Yes I do. I don't want to pretend you're someone else. I want you."

There was a long silence. "Why?"

Sarah thought about the men who'd occasionally asked her out since John died, all perfectly nice, respectable men in the community. None had raised a spark of interest in her. But from the moment she'd seen Tom and looked into his somber eyes she'd felt awakened. Alive. What she felt for him was more than physical attraction. Something unique in him called to something in her.

"I don't know why," she admitted. "It's just you. I want to be with you. I feel like we belong together." She smoothed one hand up his torso and rested it on his chest, picturing the chained heart and feeling his real heart beating steadily behind it. "Don't you?"

In answer he wrapped his arms around her, pulled her to him, and kissed her.

There was no more talking now as their mouths fused hungrily together. The lust they'd fought for days was unleashed at last.

Sarah's skin burned feverishly under Tom's touch. He ran his hands over her back, the curve of her hips and the swell of her buttocks. He pushed her underwear down and squeezed her bare bottom. Then he brushed his fingers over the crevice between her cheeks.

Her body tensed all over. Moisture gathered between

her legs and her sex throbbed as it rubbed against the bulge in his pants. She rocked against him, aroused by his ragged breathing as he responded to her movements.

Sarah climbed off his lap and removed her underpants. Tom took off his trousers and then they were both naked. She looked down at her body, a pale ghost in the dim light, and at Tom's body, dark and mysterious with an occasional flash of vibrant color when his skin caught the light. She reclined on the couch and spread her legs, her pussy wet with anticipation and her heart pounding. Tom moved on top of her, his weight supported on his arms wedged into the couch on either side of her.

The sofa was too narrow for two, but Sarah didn't want to interrupt this to go upstairs to her bedroom. Already Tom's cock was nudging at her slippery cleft and she reached down to guide him to it. She'd never been so wet and ready so quickly. He hadn't even touched her down there and she was aching for him.

Tom emitted a low groan as he slowly sheathed himself inside her.

It had been a long time since Sarah had lain with a man and she was tight. She consciously relaxed her muscles, but they still clasped around his shaft like a glove and she felt absolutely filled.

Tom slowly drew himself almost all the way out, dragging past the sensitive lips of her pussy and making her gasp. Then he thrust in again. She lifted her hips to meet him.

His pace accelerated quickly. His need was so raw she knew he wouldn't take long. Sarah wrapped her legs around his hips, anchoring him to her. She reached up and pulled his face down to hers for a kiss, then she whispered urgently, "Pull out before you release."

He grunted and after he'd plunged into her only a few more times, she felt an aching absence as he obeyed her command. He continued pumping against her pubic mound and stomach. His cock brushed over her clit with each thrust. Within seconds Sarah felt the gathering sensation of her impending climax. A million sparks coalesced at that one point then exploded through her in a shower of flames. She cried out, squeezing her legs and arms around his body and arching her pelvis off the couch.

Tom froze in his thrusting and his body shuddered in her arms. His hoarse cry cut across the saccharine melody on the radio, a raw, primitive counterpoint to the crooning singer.

His seed spurted onto her stomach, and he rocked a few more times, brushing over her sensitive clit and making her groan. Then he collapsed on top of her, breathing heavily. His back was slick with sweat under her hands and his shoulders heaved.

Sarah didn't mind his weight pinning her to the couch. It felt good to be covered, by a man's body. She couldn't stop her mind drifting to John and recalling their lovemaking. Her husband had been a gentle lover. On their wedding night he'd moved slowly, used his fingers to make her ready and prepare the way for his penetration. Then he'd entered her in careful increments until her body accepted all of him.

The sex act itself was the same, but the feeling of the two men couldn't be more different. For one thing, John was heavier while Tom was thin and wiry, his muscles coiled springs of energy. Other differences she couldn't even find words for. Contrasts of personality came through in subtle ways in their lovemaking. Where John had been open, affable and earthy, Tom's quiet intensity felt almost ethereal.

Sarah disregarded the comparisons. It was ridiculous to imagine she could tell something profound from one sexual encounter with Tom. The knowledge that there would be more encounters, that she would invite Tom into her bed and spend the rest of the night exploring his body, set her pulse racing once more.

"Shall we go to my room? It will be more comfortable."

He lifted his head to look into her eyes. They gleamed in the dim light. "Yes." The word was almost a sigh.

Chapter Six

Sarah turned off the radio and led the way upstairs, feeling Tom's eyes roving over her naked body as he followed her.Unconsciously she walked with a little twitch to her hips, and when she glanced over her shoulder, predictably his eyes were trained on her rear. She grinned at the typical male behavior. But then, if she'd been the one walking behind, she would have been gawking at his bare backside.

Her bedroom was stuffy and she opened the window to let in the night breeze. Since Tom seemed to want his privacy, she didn't turn on the light. The moonlight through the window cast everything in shades of blue, black and gray, including Tom's figure crossing the room toward her.

Sarah pulled back the covers on the bed. The moment took on a deep significance beyond the simple act. Sharing her bed with a new man would put John in her past. Her slow transition into letting him go would be finalized when she allowed Tom to take his place and sleep in their marriage bed.

Slipping between the covers, she looked at Tom and patted the bed beside her. He climbed in and lay on his side, resting his weight on one arm. In the pale moonlight, with the color leached from the patterns on his skin, he looked like a pen and ink drawing come to life.

She reached up to touch Tom's cheek and stroke her thumb over his lips. He leaned into her touch, kissed her thumb then wrapped his lips around it and sucked it into his mouth. She whimpered at the sensation of heat and wetness, and her body stirred in anticipation.

She wanted him all over again.

He let her thumb go and grasped her hand, bringing it to his mouth to kiss the back. His lips brushed seductively over her skin. Then he leaned to kiss her mouth with no hesitancy this time. He laid claim to her, swirling his tongue between her lips and kissing her deeply.

When at last he released her mouth, he trailed kisses along her jaw and throat. Sarah squirmed at his tickling lips and felt his smile against her skin. She closed her eyes and melted into pure sensation as he kissed a path down to her breasts and suckled each nipple. She arched her chest into his touch, begging for more. But he abandoned her breasts to move even lower, spreading her legs apart and kissing around her pussy and down toward her thighs.

Sarah's eyes flew open. John had ever done this. He'd primed her with his fingers, but never his tongue. She'd heard of oral sex but it wasn't something good Christian folks did. She'd never taken John's penis into her mouth either.

Now, as she looked down at Tom's head between her legs, she was about to stop him when his tongue licked between her folds and over her clit in one long stroke. She gasped. What did it matter whether wholesome people did this or not? She couldn't believe God would damn her for indulging in something that felt so good.

He delved inside her as far as he could reach, then teased and nibbled her sensitive bud until she squirmed. Her desire spiraled up and up until it burst in a cloud of exultation. Lights exploded against the dark screen of her closed eyelids when she came.

Tom moved up to lie beside her as she slowly descended back to earth. He rubbed small circles on her stomach until she subsided with a final shudder and sigh. Sarah opened her eyes and his amazing face was the first thing she saw. "That was wonderful. Thank you."

He smiled.

"Do you want me to do that for you? I haven't before, but I'm sure I can figure it out."

"No. Turn on your side."

He moved in behind her. His body curved around hers and his muscular arms pulling her tight against him. His breath tickled her shoulder and his erection rested, warm and heavy, in the groove between her buttocks. He kissed her shoulder as he began to move against her.

She loved the feeling of his cock sliding over her rear while she was held snug and secure against him. It was a very comfortable way to make love. She relaxed and let him do everything.

He fondled her breasts and kissed her shoulder and the back of her neck. Her anus clenched at the feeling of him sliding across it. His breathing grew shallower and he reached down to guide himself into her sex. She was so slick he slipped inside with ease, groaning as her warmth enveloped him.

She thrust back against him to take him deeply inside. A sense of completeness filled her, not just from the physical act but from an inexplicable sense of connection with this strange, silent man. He understood her pain and loss like no one else could, and she had no doubt he could glimpse her very thoughts and emotions with his psychic ability. It was a little frightening to be such an open book to another person, but it also took away the loneliness she'd been wearing like a dark cloak around her.

His hips pushed against her rear as he drove into her. Quiet groans and gasps escaped him as he built up speed. Their bodies slapped together faster and faster until at last Tom pulled out and spilled his seed over her lower back. He held her tight enough to bruise her ribs as he pumped against her, and he bit down on her shoulder as he came.

Afterward, he held her fast. His panting breaths sounded almost like sobs as he pressed his face into the back of her neck.

"Sarah," he whispered, and her heart clenched at the haunted sound. He rubbed her shoulder where he'd bitten it. "I'm sorry. Did I hurt you?"

"No. It's fine. Really. That was so…" Powerful didn't seem a strong enough word. Animal. Primal. Elemental. None of them covered the strength of their intimacy. "That was good."

He kissed where he'd bitten. "Sorry," he repeated.

Sarah pulled away from him to take a handkerchief

from the nightstand drawer. Feeling a little guilty about using the embroidered handkerchief her grandmother had given her, she offered it to Tom to wipe them both clean. But perhaps Grandma would understand for she'd lived and loved a man others had thought questionable. The woman had known passion in her life.

The thought made Sarah smile.

She cuddled up against Tom and rested her head on his chest. His heart still beat fast, but as she held him, it slowly diminished. She felt comfortable and so content in his warm embrace and was almost asleep when he spoke.

"You asked me about my dream, the one where I saw you. The reason I recognized you was this moment. I dreamed about it."

She was immediately wide-awake. She believed him, and his powers awed and even frightened her a little. What might he see about her life, past or present, and her private thoughts? He was so foreign in more ways than his physical appearance. But that very strangeness drew her to him. Tom was an outsider, and lately, even when she was with friends, she felt like one too.

"I'm glad," she finally said. "I'm glad you dreamed of me and that you came to me." She hugged him and kissed his chest.

"You don't mind the way I look?"

"I told you the other day you look good to me." She propped herself up on one elbow and looked in the eyes. "You're the gentlest person I've ever met. I think you're beautiful."

She was rewarded by a slow, sweet smile that utterly convinced her she hadn't made a mistake in bringing Tom into her bed and into her life. Making love to him was the best thing she'd done in a long, long time.

Chapter Seven

When Sarah woke the next morning, the sun pouring in the window blinded her. A dull ache throbbed behind her eyelids from the previous night's vodka and he neck was stiff from lying for too long with her head on Tom's chest.

Tom. A smile crept over her face as she recalled everything they'd done the previous night, and she stretched the luxuriant stretch of a woman who'd been well satisfied. She felt Tom move on the other side of the bed and turned to see if he was still asleep.

He lay sprawled on his back, eyes closed, one arm flung above his head, the other hand resting on his stomach. All the colors of his body shone in the sunlight like a jewel box spilled across her rumpled sheets.

Sarah's gaze instantly went to his penis, which she'd felt but never seen last night. She gasped when she saw Tom's semi-rigid cock resting against his stomach. Not only was it circumcised, unlike her husband's, but it was also tattooed. Wrapped around the shaft were graphically-rendered coils of barbed wire binding it from the base to the head. She thought of the hours of painful needling such a tattoo would have required and her horror at Reed's torture grew. Whether Tom had been physically restrained or submitted in order to earn food, he had not chosen to have these things done to his body. These designs had been inflicted on him.

So this was why he hadn't wanted her to see him last night. He was ashamed. She felt guilty, as if she was gawking at him in that sideshow tent all over again, yet she couldn't look away. On his thighs were rendered images of Adam and Eve. On the right, Eve reached to pluck the apple from the Tree of Knowledge. Its branches spread over his hip and groin. It was clear Eve was meant to be reaching for his genitals in a lewd parody of the Bible story. On his left leg, Adam turned away in shame, one arm covering his eyes as he was cast out of the Eden. Reed might be evil incarnate but his artistic skill was undeniable.

Tom shifted in his sleep, inhaling deeply. Sarah's eyes shot to his face. The last thing she wanted was for him to wake up and catch her staring at what he wanted to keep private. Then Tom rolled over and again she couldn't stop herself from looking at the tattoos which had been covered by his trousers. Below the ocean of fish on his back was a depiction of hell in which demons cavorted. Their actions—which carnival-goers would never see since they were hidden under a loincloth—depicted the rape and torture of screaming people. Bits of the green leaves of Eden wrapped around Tom's hips from the front, but his buttocks and the back of his thighs were covered in flames of yellow, orange and black.

Ashamed of herself for staring so long, she covered Tom's lower half with the sheet, kissed his shoulder, and got out of bed. Farm chores didn't allow for a rare day of sleeping in. Both Edison and Millie must be fed.

Sarah went through the familiar routine of pouring feed in the horse's box, pitching hay and filling water troughs, but her mind was in turmoil. Last night, under the spell of sexual heat and the influence of alcohol, she'd felt uninhibited and unashamed to fulfill her needs. But in the morning light, prohibitions instilled in her since childhood muddied her mind with doubt. Sex outside of marriage was considered a sin. She may have given up on church-going since John's death, but the rules of both church and society were ingrained. On top of that, Tom was an emotionally scarred man and socially unacceptable in her community. There were many serious issues to consider in this love affair she had hurtled into.

She was seated on the milking stool, forehead pressed against Millie's warm brown flank, milk squirting into the bucket with a metallic ping, when she heard Tom's step behind her. She looked over her shoulder at him. He stood, hands in pockets, watching her with a worried pucker between his eyebrows. Clearly he felt as uncertain about what had happened the previous night as she did.

But when Sarah smiled at him, his frown disappeared. A wide grin lit up his face and creased the corners of his eyes. "I can pitch down the hay," he offered.

"Already done and I'm almost through here, too." Sarah gave a last pull and stood, lifting the bucket from beneath the cow. "How about something to eat? I'm starving."

He reached to take the milk bucket, but Sarah placed it on the ground and took his hand. "Last night was really special. Thank you for all of it."

His shining eyes said everything. He pulled her into his arms and held her. She rested her head on his chest and breathed him in, for the moment all fears and doubts dismissed.

They returned to the house and dug into breakfast with gusto. Afterward, Sarah intended to wash the dishes while Tom took the animals out to pasture, but Tom never made it out the door. What started as a goodbye kiss ended with Sarah's housedress and apron pushed up around her waist and Tom's trousers around his ankles. He knocked the dirty dishes off the table and laid her back on the checked oilcloth, then climbed on top of her. She grappled him to her with arms and legs like bands of iron and they thrust together with ruthless fervor. They rutted like animals, rough and hungry and careless. It was exciting and Sarah thought she could happily start every day this way.

Her long sexual drought coupled with Tom's aggressive lovemaking brought her to a peak almost immediately. Sarah cried out as she came. She'd never been so noisy, so needy before. Spurred by her shout of ecstasy, Tom gave a guttural groan. He pulled out of her and shot onto her leg and across the tabletop.

Overcome by her intense orgasm and the sheer absurdity of sex itself, Sarah started to laugh. Tom looked down at her wide-eyed.

"Sorry. It's just so funny when you think about it," she gasped then broke off into another fit of giddy laughter.

He frowned.

Mindful of his male pride she said, "It's not you. I've never had such a strong climax. It was just so wonderful."

Seemingly satisfied with her explanation, he climbed off of her and the table. He pulled up his pants and gave her some of the paper napkins that had drifted to the floor. Still snickering softly, Sarah wiped up and pulled down her skirt.

When she looked at Tom, he had a mischievous glint in his eye.

"Want me to help finish clearing the dishes?" He indicated the plates, cups and silverware strewn across the floor.

She snorted with laughter. Wrapping her arms around his neck, she pulled him to her for a lingering kiss. "You can help me clear the table after every meal," she promised.

Later that morning, Sarah was in the garden cutting heads of cabbage to make into sauerkraut when she heard a car engine approaching from the road. She glanced toward the pasture where Tom was repairing a section of fence. He wasn't in view from the house or garden so he would be safe there until the visitor was gone.

The Burkett's ancient Ford truck rattled into the yard and stopped. Mary Burkett climbed out. Sarah put the cabbage in a bushel basket and walked from the garden toward the driveway.

"Howdy, neighbor! I haven't seen you in so long. We miss you at church." Mrs. Burkett offered a paper bag. "Here's a few jars of my homemade jam. There's peach, raspberry and elderberry in there."

"Thank you. Won't you come in and visit for a while?"

"Can't. I just stopped by to tell you the news. One of the Brodbeck girls, Aileen, disappeared yesterday. She went hiking in the woods in the afternoon and when she wasn't back by supper Betty started to worry. She called some of her friends but they hadn't seen her." Mary paused to draw breath. "When she wasn't back by dark, her parents called Sheriff Ziegler. A search party took Stan Jeffries' dogs into the woods, but the ground was too wet and they couldn't catch her scent. They had to call off the search 'til this morning."

"Oh no. That's terrible." Sarah pictured the freckle-faced twelve-year-old with hair as bright as a copper penny.

"They haven't found her yet. Everybody's thinking she might've been kidnapped. Stolen and *raped* or murdered by that crazy man from the carnival."

Sarah opened her mouth to protest, but Mrs. Burkett continued, "So anyway, my Charlie's out with the search party and I've got some pies to take to where the ladies are setting up lunch for them. You want to ride along?"

Sarah thought fast. She was an outsider in this community, having married into it rather than being born and bred here. Since John's death, shed' become reclusive and stopped attending church and social functions. It would be wrong not to help in this community effort to find Aileen, not to mention long-remembered that she hadn't pitched in. But she couldn't leave without explaining to Tom what was happening.

"I'm in the middle of something, but I'll bring a dish

over in about an hour. Tell the ladies I'll be there."

"We're setting up in Simpson's orchard at the edge of the state forest. That's where the girl often went walking. Oh, I hate to think of that poor child and what may have happened to her."

After her neighbor had driven away, Sarah took her basket of cabbages to the house and set them in the mud room. She chose a plump head to make into coleslaw. As she chopped and grated, she thought of the large tract of land that made up the state forest. Aileen could be anywhere, and if she was unconscious or, God forbid, dead, they might sweep past her without finding her. Sarah was worried about the girl, but also upset that people were laying blame on Tom. To them he was an axe-wielding boogeyman, a tall tale with no basis in reality. As long as he was an unknown entity, it was easy for people to place their fears on him.

Tom couldn't remain hidden forever. If he was going to stay with Sarah on a long term basis eventually he'd have to be introduced to the community. But when? There would never be a good time.

Lost in thought, Sarah's hand slipped and she scraped her knuckles on the grater. Blood welled. She cursed and put her hand under the tap, letting cold water soothe her torn flesh. As she patted blood away with a paper towel, she thought of other blood, menstrual blood, and wondered if interruption was a safe enough birth control method. With John she'd not had to worry about preventing pregnancy since they were trying to have a child. Now it was a big problem. If she and Tom were going to continue having intercourse, she should drive to the city to buy protection. She certainly couldn't get condoms at the pharmacy in Fairfield without drawing attention.

The back door opened and closed and Tom's boots clomped into the entry. She turned as he appeared in the kitchen doorway. "That was my neighbor in the truck. She stopped by to tell me about a little girl who's missing."

"She's hurt."

Sarah felt as if the air had been sucked from the kitchen and she was suddenly aware of the ticking of the clock on the wall. "What?"

He stood behind one of the kitchen chairs, hands resting on the back. "She's somewhere dark." His eyes went unfocussed, gazing through Sarah rather than at her. "And her leg hurts so badly she thinks it's broken."

The hair on her neck prickled and rose.

"She's screaming for help." His voice was detached as if he were describing a picture.

"You see this right now? You see Aileen?"

He continued as if he hadn't heard her, "She's afraid no one will ever find her and she'll die there alone. She wants to go home."

Sarah took a deep breath and collected her panicked thoughts. "Okay. So if you're getting impressions of her, she's alive. Can you see the place she's at?"

He gripped the chair and swayed slightly, his gaze drilling through the wall. "Small. Dark. No air."

"She's trapped somewhere? Do you see anything that could give a clue where she is?"

He frowned. "Stone. Rocks. Dirt." There was a long pause. His eyes scanned back and forth as if reading an invisible book then suddenly blinked and focused on Sarah. "That's all."

Adrenaline rushed through her veins leaving her shaken. She realized she was still clutching the bloodied paper towel in one fist and she set it on the counter. She tried to gather her wits and shut out her primitive fear of the unknown. There must be a practical way to use Tom's gift to locate the girl. "Are your visions only sensations or pictures too?"

"Sometimes both."

"Do you think you might get a stronger impression if you saw Aileen's photo?"

"I don't know. I've never tried to see these things. They just come."

She bit her lip. "But you could try. It might make a difference. We have to go to the sheriff. We have to try to help find this girl."

He looked down at his hands for a long moment then back up at her. "All right."

Sarah took one of his hands and squeezed it. "I'll be with you the whole time. It will be all right. I'll make the sheriff listen to what you have to say."

He looked into her eyes with his profound gaze and nodded.

She realized how much trust she was demanding of him. "You'll be safe."

Sarah slipped on a jacket and got the keys to the Plymouth. As Tom slid in beside her, she saw him as others would. He wore John's dark jeans, chambray work shirt and navy jacket, clothing any man around here might wear. But Tom looked like an alien being with his head and hands tattooed in those swirling blue designs. She considered offering him a cap to wear but thought it might come across as if she was ashamed of his appearance.

Tom sat in the passenger seat, staring at his hands resting in his lap. She reached over and touched his forearm. "It'll be okay."

He looked at her, then grabbed her arm and pulled her to him. He gave her a lingering kiss before letting her go. It felt as if he was saying goodbye.

"Don't worry. Everything will be fine," she reassured him—and herself—yet again.

He looked out the side window.

Sarah put the car in gear and drove toward town. After several miles of tense silence, she turned on the radio and nervously tapped her fingers on the steering wheel in time with the Glenn Miller Band.

She stopped the car in front of the sheriff's office and turned to Tom. "Why don't you stay here? Sheriff Ziegler is probably out with the searchers, but I want to check here first and, if he's there, explain who you are."

She got out and closed the car door behind her. Tom scooted down in the seat as low as he could.

The sheriff's office consisted of a front room with a couple of desks, the sheriff's private office and a couple of jail cells in back.

Ziegler's wife, Anna, who acted as receptionist,

dispatcher and secretary, sat at one of the desks talking on the two-way radio.

"Hold on a minute Jack. Somebody just came in." She tapped a switch and the static buzz of the radio went dead. "Hello, Mrs. Cassidy, I suppose you heard about Aileen."

"Yes. That's why I'm here." Sarah exhaled, trying to find the right words to present her case without sounding crazy. She didn't know Anna very well, but had the impression the woman was a practical person. Hopefully she would listen without judging.

"I have something to tell the sheriff. It's kind of strange, but may be useful in finding Aileen. I'd like to talk to him privately if possible—not in front of an entire search party. I don't suppose you could have him meet me here."

Mrs. Ziegler cocked her head and looked at Sarah curiously through her thick glasses. "What's your information?"

Sarah forced herself to relax and not clasp her hands together like an anxious schoolgirl. "It's more of a premonition really. A friend's premonition, not mine, but he's very reliable." Noting the woman's skeptical expression, Sarah added, "I know it sounds nuts but he honestly has a gift. I thought if he could look at a photo of Aileen or touch something of hers..." She trailed off, her face burning.

Mrs. Ziegler tapped a pen against the tablet of paper in front of her. "Who is this friend?"

"Oh, golly." Sarah laughed nervously. "Here's the problem. My friend is the man from the carnival they've been looking for." She took a step toward the desk and began speaking quickly. "But he's not dangerous or retarded like people think. That man who owns the carnival kept him basically a prisoner for most of his life. I didn't tell the sheriff or deputy about it before because Tom was afraid they might try to return him to Reed. I know this all sounds absolutely insane, but it's the truth. If I could talk to your husband privately about all of this, I know I could make him understand. Tom, that's the man's name, has these visions sometimes and he saw that Aileen was hurt and trapped somewhere dark and—"

Mrs. Ziegler held up her hand and interrupted. "He *saw* her? When was this?"

"No, not saw her physically, but in his head. It was this morning, I guess. At least that's when he told me about it."

"Where is this man now?"

"Out in the car waiting. I thought it would be better if I talked to someone first."

"Can you get him to come in here?"

"Of course. That's what we came for, so he could talk to Sheriff Ziegler and tell him about the, ah, vision." Sarah swallowed the last word in an embarrassed mumble.

"Mrs. Cassidy, why don't you go get the man and I'll radio Jack."

As Sarah turned to obey, Mrs. Ziegler spoke into the handset. "Uh, Jack, you there? I've got somebody here you're going to want to talk to."

Outside the sidewalk was empty. The town appeared deserted since most people had gone to join in the search. Sarah was grateful for that. For a second as she peered into the dim interior of the car, it looked like Tom was no longer there. He had pressed himself back into the seat and was slouched down so far he was almost invisible.

Sarah opened the car door. "Are you ready to come in? The sheriff is going to talk to you."

Tom's jaw was tight and his lips compressed in a straight line, but he nodded and got out of the car.

As she walked with him into the building, Sarah felt as if she was leading an innocent animal to slaughter. Alarm bells clanged in her head telling her that this heartfelt effort to help would somehow end up with Tom behind bars. But now that she'd started the process, she didn't know how to stop it. All she could do was try to make the sheriff listen and believe.

Mrs. Ziegler looked curiously at Tom then adopted a neutral expression. "Why don't you two take a seat until Jack gets here? Can I get you a cup of coffee or some iced tea?"

Sarah admired the woman's aplomb. "Iced tea would be nice. Thank you." She and Tom sat down in a pair of scarred, wooden chairs with no padding in the waiting area along one wall.

Mrs. Ziegler went into the back and came out with a thermos and a pair of coffee mugs. "This should still be cold. Fresh from my refrigerator this morning." She poured and passed them the tea, studying the sun on the back of Tom's hand as he accepted his cup. She perched on the edge of the desk facing them and sipped from her own mug.

"I know it's not my business to ask questions, but do you want to tell me what's going on?"

"It's exactly like I said." Sarah retold Tom's story,

adding her experience of nearly getting crushed under the Plymouth to give credibility to his psychic abilities.

When she was finished, Mrs. Ziegler regarded Tom thoughtfully. "Well, I've heard stranger tales. Not much stranger, mind you. Truth to tell, I've read about this kind of thing before, somebody with visions solving a case no one else could. Of course that was in a pulp magazine but still, I guess anything is possible."

Sarah relaxed slightly for the first time since she'd entered the office.

The phone rang and the Anna set down her mug and stood. "I have to say, it would have made things a whole lot easier if you'd have come in right away and told Jack your story about this carnival fellow Reed. Jack and Phil wasted a lot of man-hours this past week beating the bush and going door to door trying to find *him*," she nodded at Tom. "Jack's in kind of a sour mood so he may tear into you. But don't you mind his yelling. He hasn't had enough sleep and it makes him cranky."

She went to answer the ringing telephone. "Endora County Sheriff's Office."

Sitting in the straight-backed chairs waiting for Sheriff Ziegler to arrive, Sarah felt like a naughty child waiting to face the school principal. She considered numerous ways of telling the story that might make it sound more reasonable and her actions logical, when from the moment she'd met Tom, she'd been reacting with her heart instead of her head. She looked over at him.

His hands were clasped in his lap, clenching and

unclenching.

She rubbed his arm and gave him an encouraging smile. When she glanced at Mrs. Ziegler, the woman was still talking on the phone but watching them speculatively.

After ten minutes the sheriff's cruiser pulled up outside. Sheriff Ziegler stomped through the door and straight over to Sarah and Tom. He stood before them, legs apart, arms folded over his considerable gut and a scowl on his face. He nodded at Sarah. "Mrs. Cassidy." Then his gaze settled on Tom.

Tom sat up even straighter in his chair. Sarah could almost feel the tension vibrating through him.

"And who is this?"

Sarah answered for him. "Tom."

"Well, I wasted a lot of my time over the past week searching for you, Tom. Why the blazes didn't you come in right away?"

"He hasn't broken any laws and he didn't feel he could trust the authorities to recognize his rights as a fully sound and functional individual."

Ziegler continued to address Tom. "And now you come forward with some story about Aileen Brodbeck, who just happened to disappear since you came into the area."

"I know it seems strange but—"

"Can the man speak for himself, Mrs. Cassidy?" the sheriff snapped. "I have to look at him as a suspect in this disappearance. By all rights I should have him in handcuffs by now."

"No! We came here in good faith that you would hear

what Tom has to say with an open mind. He only came because I told him it would be safe."

"So far I haven't heard the man say a single word on his own behalf. All's I know is we have a little girl missing and a stranger who apparently knows something about it." He glared at Sarah. "Can you vouch for his whereabouts yesterday? I heard through the grapevine you were over in Camden with Andrew Harper and the Cunninghams all evening. Who was watching your friend then? Damnation, I ought to be arresting you too for harboring a fugitive and obstructing justice," Ziegler's voice rose.

"Don't!" Tom shouted.

Sarah jumped.

"Don't yell at her." He was poised on the edge of his seat, eyes narrowed, hands clenched on the armrests as though ready to launch himself at the sheriff. He looked angry and dangerous, nothing like the gentle, quiet man she'd come to know over the past days. He certainly didn't seem to be the non-violent person she was trying to represent to Sheriff Ziegler.

After a moment of silence, the sheriff said mildly, "So you *can* speak. Hell's bells, son, relax. I'm not going to arrest either one of you. Not yet anyway. If Mrs. Cassidy here vouches for you, I suppose that'll do—for now. But you damn sure better believe I have some questions." He yelled to his wife though she was only a few feet away, "Anna, you want to bring me a glass of iced tea?"

"We're out." She sighed and rose from her seat. "But I suppose I could walk over to the drugstore and get you a Pepsi

Cola. Cool you down before you pop a blood vessel." She gathered her purse and jacket and left the office.

Ziegler sat on the edge of the desk facing them as his wife had done earlier. "All right, why don't you tell me everything you know about the missing girl."

Tom was still perched on his chair like a wild creature ready to run—or attack. His gaze was riveted on the sheriff, watching his every move.

Sarah squeezed his arm. "It's all right," she whispered and felt his muscles relax slightly. She addressed the sheriff. "Look, I know this is hard to believe, but Tom gets flashes of ... I guess you'd call it insight about people. The second day he was at my house I was draining the oil on my Plymouth and he pulled me out from under just before it fell off the jack. He said he saw it happen in his head. He saved my life."

"That true?" Ziegler stared Tom in the eye.

"Yes."

"Can you tell me what you know about Aileen?"

When Sarah opened her mouth, Ziegler held up his hand to silence her. "I'd like to hear it from him."

Tom spoke quietly. "She's trapped someplace dark and rocky, under the earth. There's hardly any air. Her leg is hurt. And she's afraid. That's all I felt."

Ziegler frowned. "Well, that doesn't give me a lot to go on, now does it?"

Sarah broke in. "That's why I thought it might help if he could look at her picture or hold something of hers. I know it sounds crazy but isn't it worth a try?"

The sheriff rocked back on the desk and it creaked

under his weight. He stared hard at Tom for several long seconds, then he stood up, scattering papers from the desk to the floor.

"Why not. Couldn't hurt." He looked into Tom's eyes again. "But you'd better be prepared for this. We got a whole lot of people who've imagined you into the worst kind of monster. It ain't going to be friendly out there. Are you ready for that?"

Tom nodded. "Yes. I want to help the girl."

Chapter Eight

When they arrived at Simpson's orchard in the squad car, it looked more like a community picnic going on than a search operation. Children chased one another in games of tag around the gnarled apple trees or snatched food off the heavily laden tables. Clusters of men and women from town and area farms stood talking and eating. Sarah saw Grace May cutting a cake at one of the tables. Andrew and Mike stood in a group with Mr. McNulty, the hardware store owner, and several other merchants.

Deputy Phil talked earnestly with Aileen's parents, Glenn and Betty and her older sister, Shirley. The younger Brodbeck children yelled and ran with the rest of the kids unmindful of the gravity of the situation. Glenn's arm was around Betty's shoulders and she looked ready to collapse if he let go.

Sarah prayed there was something useful Tom could offer these parents besides the knowledge that their daughter was trapped, hurt and afraid.

"All right, folks, here goes," Sheriff Ziegler opened the door of the cruiser, swung his legs out and hoisted himself up with the aid of the door frame. "Stay by me and let me do the talking." He looked at Sarah as she emerged from the vehicle. "That means you."

They followed the sheriff across the grass to where Aileen's parents stood. When people noticed Tom, they fell silent or whispered to one another as they stared at him. Acutely aware of their disapproval, Sarah was glad to walk in Ziegler's substantial shadow. Being the center of attention of almost an entire town was intimidating. Even the children stopped their play to gape at the tattooed man walking freely under the sun instead of contained in a carnival tent. Grace May's mouth literally dropped open in surprise, and Andrew and Mike wore equally shocked expressions.

"Phil," Ziegler said to his deputy as they drew close. "I want you to circulate among these people and tell them this man isn't a danger to anybody. He's got some information that might prove useful. That's all they need to know about it. Lay their minds to rest and calm them down. Got it?"

The deputy's eyes popped as he looked from Tom to Sarah and back again. "Uh, sure thing, Jack." He moved dutifully away.

Ziegler took one of Betty Brodbeck's hands in his big fist. "Betty, Glenn, I want you to meet Tom. He's the fellow from the carnival everyone's been so worked up about."

The distraught parents stared uncomprehendingly at the incongruous sight of the carnival freak in Simpson's orchard.

"Tom here claims to have some ... special abilities, like what they used to call the second sight. I know a lot of folks don't take stock in that. I don't much myself, but I figured what the hell, might be worth a shot if he could help find Aileen."

Glenn stared at Tom suspiciously. "I don't think—"

"Yes," Betty spoke over him, looking directly into Tom's eyes through her red-rimmed ones. "We'll try anything to find her. Anything. What do we need to do?"

"Do you have her picture with you?" Sarah asked.

The woman reached into the pocket of her dress and drew out a photo. Tears filled her eyes as she looked at it then handed it to Tom.

It was a school photo of a freckle-faced girl with a huge smile and long coppery pigtails, one starting just above her ear, the other at least two inches higher.

"That's last year's," Betty said softly. "They haven't had picture day at school yet this year. Aileen's a head taller now and starting to look so grown up."

Tom stared intently at the picture in his hand for several moments then closed his eyes. They all waited, watching him expectantly. In the distance, Sarah was dimly aware of murmuring voices like bees buzzing around the fallen apples beneath the trees. She prayed hard for Tom to see something useful.

But after a moment he opened his eyes, looked at the picture again and shook his head. "I'm sorry. I only get the same thing as before. She's stuck somewhere dark and earthy and her leg hurts."

Betty let out a small cry and covered her mouth with a hand. Her husband gazed, narrow-eyed at Tom like he was a puzzle he couldn't quite figure out. "You see that? You really see her?"

Tom shook his head. "No. It's like I feel what she's feeling."

Sarah touched his arm. "The rocks. You said before that there were rocks." She turned to the sheriff. "Is there someplace rocky around here, a well, a cave, a mine? Anyplace a child might crawl into and get stuck."

Ziegler shook his head. "No mining ever done around these parts I'm aware of and I've lived here all of my life. No caves either so far as I know."

"Could there be a boarded-over well?" Betty said. "We've been looking so hard in the forest we may be missing someplace else."

Sarah pictured rotten boards giving away under running feet and a little girl plunging thirty or forty feet down to the bottom. How could she survive it?

"Do you have any of her possessions with you?" she asked.

"Here," Aileen's sister, Shirley held out a red cardigan. "This is hers. They let the dogs smell it yesterday before they went out. The deputy just gave it to me to take home." She turned to her mother. "I read about this stuff in Amazing Stories, mom. Sometimes it really works."

Tom accepted the sweater, stroking his moon hand over the soft material. Again everyone in the little group went still, watching him. He glanced at Betty's harrowed face then back down at the sweater. His jaw clenched and his brows furrowed in concentration.

Sarah sensed his frustration and fear of not being able to help. She laid her hand over his on the sweater. "Don't try so hard," she whispered. "Relax and let it come to you like before."

He nodded and exhaled audibly. Smoothing his hand over the sweater, he almost visibly relaxed, shoulders dropping and eyes partially closing. Several long moments of silence followed.

Sarah glanced around the orchard and saw Phil talking to an irate group of people whose voices were growing steadily louder. She looked back at Tom in time to see his face go slack, his eyes tracking back and forth like they had earlier. He was entering that eerie trancelike state. She wasn't surprised when he suddenly began to speak.

"She's walking." His voice was low and level, no inflection disturbing the halting recitation. Finds a ... a place and goes inside. It's dark."

The hair on Sarah's arms rose and a glance at the others showed they were equally mesmerized.

"She wishes she had a flashlight, wishes her friend Katie was with her."

"Ziegler! What the heck is going on?" An angry voice broke the spell. The town barber, Aaron Avery, marched up to the sheriff and pointed at Tom. "What is *he* doing here?"

"Damn it, Avery," Ziegler snapped. "Didn't Phil tell all of you this man's helping with the investigation? Back off and let him do his ... job."

"And what *is* that? We've walked acres of that forest without seeing hide nor hair of the girl. What does this freak know about where she's at?"

Other men and women had gathered behind Avery, drawn by curiosity and the desire to be part of the drama.

"Where has he been all this time?" Mrs. Davidson called out. "Where's he been hiding?" She gave Sarah a meaningful look.

"And why was he hiding?" another woman chimed in, "If he hasn't done anything wrong, why's he been skulking around instead of coming forward to face folks."

"Well, he's facing folks now, isn't he? And look how well *that's* turning out," Ziegler said dryly. "Look, I realize you all have a lot of questions and I'll explain everything later, but right now the important thing is using any means possible to find Aileen."

"What means is that? Some hoo-doo nonsense?" Avery scoffed.

"Back off, Avery," Glenn Brodbeck suddenly exploded. "It's our daughter missing and if this man can do anything at all to help, it's worth a shot."

"It's bull crap, is what it is," Avery mumbled.

Ziegler spoke loudly to the small mob that had gathered. "Like I said, all your concerns will be addressed later. We can even call a town meeting to discuss it if that'll satisfy everybody. But for now please give us some space here!"

"What about the search?" A man said. "People were just getting ready to go back out again. Are you telling us to wait now?"

"No, not at all. There's no reason to stop what you all

have already been doing. Phil, why don't you send folks back out to their sections. You got more of those tags for marking off the areas that have been covered?"

There was a flurry of activity as Phil got the people to disperse and the searchers to trek back out into the woods. Sarah watched Tom throughout the altercation. His hands grasped the sweater and he seemed oblivious of the dispute and the commotion around him as he concentrated.

"What do you see?" Betty stepped close to him and looked into his scanning eyes. "Tell me."

He frowned then his eyes focused on her. "We should start from your yard. I might be able to follow her trail." His voice was suddenly sharply decisive. "She's in a hollowed out bit of ground, not very deep. She went in to explore and it collapsed."

Tom turned to the sheriff and said with authority, "You'll need men and shovels to dig with."

"Okay. But where?"

"I don't know yet, but it's not where you have them looking."

Tom's confident tone amazed Sarah. His shy demeanor had vanished and he was completely altered from the nearly mute man she'd met a little over a week ago. She felt she was seeing the man he would have been if given a normal life.

Andrew Harper, who'd been lingering and listening on the periphery of the group, spoke up, "Sheriff, I can get shovels from the hardware store and some guys to help."

"Good," Ziegler nodded. "You do that. Get four or five men who can keep a level head and work hard and bring 'em to the Brodbeck's place, since it seems that's our starting point." Sarah was surprised at his open-mindedness in acting on Tom's input.

"Yes, sir." Before he left, Andrew made quick eye contact with Sarah. She wondered what he was thinking about her and Tom.

Betty put her daughter, Shirley in charge of looking after her younger siblings. Then the Brodbecks, Ziegler, Sarah and Tom walked through the orchard, squashing deadfall apples underfoot and releasing their fermented aroma.

The Brodbecks' property was on the east side of the orchard beyond which the forest sprawled. The search party had been focused on the forest because Aileen had said she'd be hiking there, not an uncommon pastime for the older children in the area. The kids all knew the rules and rarely went off trails and got lost.

When they reached the perimeter of the Brodbecks' back yard, Tom looked around while still gently kneading the red sweater. He scanned the lawn and trees and the field beyond then pointed west. "That way."

Betty frowned. "Are you sure? Aileen said—"

"That way," he insisted.

Tom strode along the property line then angled across the stubble of the harvested field toward the nearest county road. He walked quickly and soon the slower members of the group, Betty and the overweight sheriff, were hard-pressed to keep up, stumbling over the muddy furrows.

After following the paved road for about a hundred yards, Tom abruptly veered off the road and down an embankment. A small creek flowed from the culvert beneath the road. He followed the water's course through dense undergrowth. The ground grew marshy underfoot and their shoes mud-caked. Branches whipped their faces and briars caught at their clothes, but Tom was relentless in his course.

Glenn kept up with Tom's rapid pace, staying right on his heels. Sarah lagged a little behind them, dodging branches and sidestepping the worst of the sucking mud. The others were even farther back.

When the two men suddenly stopped, Sarah plowed into Glenn's back. They were facing the wall of a shallow ravine through which the stream ran. A steep, tree-studded incline rose before them. Green light sifted through leafy branches and a thick carpet of fallen leaves cushioned their feet. Huge rocks jutted out of the slope here and there, and lush ferns grew in the shade.

The others came panting up beside Sarah.

"What?" the sheriff asked.

"I don't know," she answered.

Tom stood holding the red sweater and turning slowly like a weather vane signaling a change in the wind. The rest of them watched him and listened, trying to catch the faintest sound of a young girl's cry for help.

Finally he stopped turning, raised his hand and pointed. "There."

They walked over to the earthy wall he'd indicated. Underneath a ledge of rock about three feet above the forest floor was a fall of rubble and dirt that could have been fresh or have lain undisturbed for years. Nothing would have attracted the attention of anyone searching the area.

Without a word Tom went to his knees in front of the pile and began throwing aside rocks and digging loose earth with his hands. After a moment's pause, the others followed his lead. Sheriff Ziegler called Phil on his walkie-talkie and told him where to direct the digging crew and to get Dr. Hunter and an ambulance to the county road.

Sarah knelt and dug beside Tom, scraping her hands on the rocks. Soon her hands were cracked and sore from the tiny abrasions, but her spirits lifted with each bit of earth or stone they removed. Surely the would reach Aileen in time, otherwise why would God have given Tom his vision?

The searchers dug for several minutes when Tom suddenly stopped. He was on his hands and knees, head bowed, struggling for breath. When he lifted his sweaty face, a trickle of blood ran from his nose. He wiped it away with the back of his hand, smearing dirt and blood.

Sarah grasped his shoulder. "Are you all right?"

He gasped for air but resumed pawing at the earth.

"What is it?" she said urgently. "What's happening?"

He whispered, "She's running out of air. We have to hurry."

Sarah's pulse raced and she redoubled her efforts. Her hands were raw and aching, but finding Aileen only to lose her was not an option. They must get to her in time.

Betty called out a steady stream of encouragement. "Aileen, can you hear me? It's mom. We're here, sweetheart. We'll get you out. Just hold on!"

Glenn didn't call to his daughter but dug with single-minded intensity, dirt flying from his fists as if they were spades.

They'd come unprepared, bringing no shovels, but couldn't have used them anyway since they might have broken through and struck the girl. As they tunneled further under the rocky outcropping, there wasn't room for more than a few people to work shoulder to shoulder. The sheriff urged Betty to rest and took her place. Soon Sarah too was bumped aside as the three men burrowed beneath the rock.

She crawled out of the confined space, brushed dirt from her knees and flexed her stiff fingers. She held Betty's hand as they watched the men move the earth to save Aileen.

Sarah didn't know how much time passed when she heard approaching voices and bodies crashing through the woods near the stream. Seconds later the clearing was filled with a half dozen men armed with shovels.

The sheriff backed out of the chasm and soon Andrew, Mike and Frank Seeber, the mechanic had taken the other men's places, digging with their hands. The men with shovels moved the piles of dirt and rock away from the entrance. The ambulance driver and Dr. Hunter stood waiting with a stretcher.

Glenn and Tom collapsed near Betty and Sarah and watched anxiously as the newcomers worked. A couple of the men began to argue whether to try to attack the cave-in with shovels or continue to tunnel with their hands when suddenly Andrew gave a muffled yell of surprise. "Hey! I'm through."

A girl's hysterical crying came from the dark hole.

"Aileen!" Betty jumped to her feet. Shoving the men

out of her way, she fell to her knees in front of the tunnel. Frank and Mike crawled out and seconds later Andrew emerged.

"I can't pull her out. Her leg's trapped under something."

Glenn wiggled into the fissure to try to free her. It had become a one-person job and all the rest of them could do was wait.

Tears streaming down her face, Betty continued to call encouragement to her daughter. "I'm here, honey. I'm here."

Sarah's own cheeks were wet and she was barely breathing as she imagined the horror of being buried alive for hours, not knowing if anyone would ever find you.

When Glen finally emerged, dragging his daughter's body, a cheer went up from the rescue party. Every inch of the girl was covered in mud. Aileen sobbed and clung to her mother, who hugged her tightly.

Sarah looked over at Tom and reached for his hand. His face was dirt-streaked. Blood still dripped from his nose, but when she touched him, he smiled at her.

The doctor examined Aileen's leg and pronounced it possibly fractured. He applied a makeshift splint before the ambulance driver and Mike Cunningham carefully lifted her onto the stretcher. She screamed despite their attempt to handle her gently.

Two men hoisted the stretcher and others went ahead to clear a path for them along the stream. The Brodbecks walked behind the stretcher and the other men trailed after. Soon the only people who remained near the cave-in were

Andrew, Sheriff Ziegler, Sarah and Tom.

The sheriff blew a long breath and wiped his sweaty face as he watched the last of the men leave. He looked at Tom. "Good work. You saved her life."

Andrew's gaze went to Sarah and Tom's clasped hands. He stared hard for a moment then stooped to collect the abandoned shovels.

Ziegler clapped Andrew on the back. "Thanks to you too, Harper, for organizing those guys."

"Glad to do it."

They continued to gather the shovels and talk, while Sarah turned to Tom.

"Are you all right? You look terrible."

"My head hurts a little," he admitted

She guessed it hurt a lot more than 'a little.' His eyes were bloodshot and the bits of his skin not covered in ink were pale, but at least his nose had stopped bleeding.

"We'll get you home and you can have a hot bath and some aspirin. You did an amazing, wonderful thing today."

He smiled slightly but shook his head.

"You did! You were a hero."

"It won't matter to them. Those people. They still won't want me here."

Sarah grasped Tom's hand. Their dry, dirt-encrusted hands slid together and the warmth and life pulsing under his skin sent a bolt of electricity through her.

Sheriff Ziegler cleared his throat. "Are you coming?"

Sarah realized they'd stood too long holding hands and gazing into each other's eyes. Both Andrew and Ziegler were watching them. She headed for the path, embarrassed to meet their eyes, although she had no reason to feel ashamed. And this was only beginning. There would be many more sidelong glances and disapproving eyes in her future with Tom by her side.

Chapter Nine

Sarah's legs felt heavy and numb as she trudged the long path back to the road, but Tom's bowed head and slight stagger signaled his exhaustion was much worse. She couldn't imagine the effort of mind and will it had taken for him to tap into his psychic power and force it to work for him.

When they reached the road, the ambulance had gone. Mike leaned against his car waiting for them. "Phil's gone to tell the searchers Aileen's been found and her parents rode to the hospital in the ambulance. I figured you all could use a ride back."

Ziegler hefted his bulk into the passenger seat next to Mike, forcing the other three to share the back. Sitting between Tom and Andrew was extremely awkward. Sarah folded her hands in her lap and stared at them, acutely aware of the men on either side of her.

"So, are you going to introduce us to your friend, Sarah?" Mike asked.

"This is Tom. Tom, these are my friends, Mike Cunningham and Andrew Harper." Observing the social niceties in such a strange situation felt bizarre.

BONE DEEP

After a moment's silence, nosy Mike started in again. "You want to tell us a little more, Sarah?"

She sighed. Now that the crisis of the missing child was over, everyone's attention would turn toward Tom. People were going to want an explanation. She would have to tell his story over and over again.

"The morning after the carnival left I found Tom in my loft. Arthur Reed had kept him a prisoner most of his life. I've let him stay at the farm while he figures out what he wants to do next. That's really all there is to it." She was pleased. It was brief, to the point and explained all people needed to know.

Mike looked at her in the rearview mirror. "What about all this mind stuff? How does that work?"

Even though the proof of Tom's power had been exhibited to everybody, Sarah felt ridiculous explaining the phenomenon. "He sees flashes, sometimes impressions of what people are feeling and sometimes images from their lives. When he told me today he'd seen Aileen trapped someplace. I took him to the sheriff, and you know the rest."

She glanced at Andrew sitting ramrod straight and listening intently to her story, and at Tom, scrunched down in his seat, staring out the window, his mind seemingly a million miles away.

"Can I ask why you didn't tell Grace and me about this?" Mike asked.

Sarah wanted to snap *Because it was none of your business.* "I don't know."

Sheriff Ziegler, who had been unusually quiet,

suddenly spoke up. "Well, this is an unusual situation, but it seems your friend here is in his right mind and no crimes have been committed, except maybe by that carnival fellow. If you want to press charges against Reed, I can call over to Hooperstown and have him taken in for questioning."

"No." Tom turned from the window, clearly more aware of the conversation than he'd let on. "No. Let it go."

Ziegler turned to look at him over the seat. "If what you say is true, I'd think you'd want some justice."

"It doesn't matter," he said quietly.

"Yes, it does," Sarah argued. "Reed should pay for what he did. He should be in jail. Why wouldn't you want to have him arrested?"

Tom's clenched his jaw and stared out the window again. "Other people depend on the carnival. It's their lives. Without it, without him, they have no work, no place to go."

Sarah pictured the rest of the so-called freaks and the barkers who operated games and rides. The carnival was a little world all of its own, and she understood Tom's reluctance to destroy it. "But Reed's a monster. He shouldn't be allowed to get away with everything he's done."

Tom looked at Ziegler and said firmly, "No. I don't want to press charges."

Everyone fell silent. A few minutes later Mike pulled in behind the other cars and pickups parked at the edge of the orchard. People were still milling around discussing everything that had happened. The last thing she wanted was to have their attention turned on Tom who needed to go home and rest.

"Mike, will you take us to my car? It's at the sheriff's office."

"Sure thing."

Andrew and Ziegler got out of the car. The sheriff leaned to talk to them through the window. "Call me if you have any trouble out at your place. You know the kind of trouble I mean."

"Thank you." Sarah tried to imagine the townsfolk with pitchforks and torches and thought that was a little extreme. They were reasonable, civilized people after all. They might not like Tom being in their community but they wouldn't come to drive him out.

Tom drove on to Main Street and when he dropped them off by the Plymouth, Sarah said, "Thanks for the ride, and please tell Grace I'm sorry about keeping secrets. Tell her to come over soon and we can talk about everything, okay?"

Mike smiled. "Don't worry, Red, we're not mad at you, and if you need help with anything let us know. Like if Tom here needs a place to stay, maybe he could come to our house for a while."

Sarah understood his message. A single woman living alone with a man was unacceptable even if the relationship was innocent. She was risking her reputation letting Tom stay at the farm, and that a reputation was something that could never be replaced once it was lost.

When Sarah pulled her car into the driveway, Tom was asleep, hunched in his corner of the front seat. She hated to wake him and when she shook his shoulder and called his name, she actually had trouble rousing him.

His long lashes fluttered and he stared at her blankly for a moment. Then recognition flooded them and he smiled. "I thought, maybe I dreamed you."

"Nope. I'm here. Flesh and blood." She massaged his shoulder, leaving dirt on his shirt. She touched his cheek with her filthy fingers then leaned in to kiss him lightly. "I'm very real."

He sat up and pulled her close, nuzzling the curve of her neck. They cuddled and kissed for several minutes before Sarah finally pushed Tom away with a smile.

"Time to clean up."

They washed away the worst of the dirt at the old hand pump in the yard, stripping off most of their filthy clothes and rinsing faces and arms before going into the house.

Upstairs in the bathroom, Sarah set water running in the tub. She took off her underclothes, enjoying how Tom's gaze swept over her body and told her silently how beautiful he thought she was.

She went to him and ran her finger along the waistband of his boxers. "We could take a bath together. Tub's big enough." She hooked the edge of his underwear and started to pull them down.

Tom grabbed her wrist.

"It's all right. I've already seen it." She kissed his chest right in the center of the chained heart. "You have nothing to hide from me."

He frowned but let go of her hand. "When did you see?"

"This morning, while you were sleeping. You were naked. It was kind of hard *not* to look." She ran her finger back and forth under the waistband.

"You don't mind it?"

"No. I told you before, I think you're beautiful." She reached her hand inside the boxers and caressed his hard, smooth shaft. "Everywhere."

She tugged down the boxers one-handed. "All of you."

His cock sprang free and thrust before him. "Every bit."

She dropped to her knees and pulled his underwear the rest of the way off, then straightened so her face was level with his cock. She glanced up and Tom was staring down with awestruck eyes. "I want to show you how *much* I like it."

She wrapped a hand around his cock and brought the tip to her mouth. She slid her tongue over the satiny head of his penis and rolled her tongue all around it, tasting the salty, musky flavor. Her pulse beat fast as she took him into her mouth.

Tom gasped loudly.

I must be doing it right. Her nervousness at trying something new disappeared as instinct took control. She sucked him in farther and moved her fist up and down his length. She worked him steadily, sucking, stroking, savoring the texture and taste of his flesh. In the background, water splashed into the tub and rising steam filled the small room. The floor was hard against her knees even through the bathmat. Details etched themselves into her consciousness: the chill of the floor, the splash of the water, the warmth of Tom's body, his soft groan of pleasure. This moment was hers forever.

The green leaves of the Tree of Knowledge spread across Tom's groin. Dark pubic hair which was beginning to grow in obscured some of the foliage. Sarah suddenly understood Reed had kept Tom clean-shaven everywhere the better to display his artwork for high paying customers. The thought made her sick.

At the corner of her vision Eve's hand reached toward Tom's testicles. Sarah cupped them herself, fondling his sac. Submissively kneeling at her lover's feet, a sense of power filled her. Her hands and mouth controlled his pleasure. She sucked hard before allowing most of his glistening length to slip from her mouth. She nibbled and kissed his head then sat back on her heels and simply gazed at his cock, the engorged head and the pulsing shaft wrapped in inked barbed wire.

He thrust his hips forward, begging her take him back in hand and reached to touch her head, urging her toward him. On trembling legs, his cock vibrating, Tom practically whimpered his need for more. She took pity on him, once more grasping him in her fist and enveloping him in her mouth.

After only a few moments of Sarah sucking and pulling, Tom suddenly grasped her head and strained into her mouth. His cock nearly gagged her as he released with a strangled cry.

Warmth hit the back of her throat and she swallowed reflexively. When his cock finished pulsing, she let it go and sat back on her heels. Wiping her hand across her lips, she looked up at his blissful expression, eyes closed and mouth gasping. Smug pride filled her. She had given him that ecstasy.

Sarah stood and wrapped her arms around him. They clung together until she glanced past Tom's shoulder and noticed the bath water creeping alarmingly high. She turned off the tap and released some water down the drain before stepping into the tub and offering her hand to Tom.

Together they reclined in the bath, Sarah between Tom's legs with her back against his front. Steamy warmth engulfed her. The ends of her hair floated in dark red swirls. Tom coiled and uncoiled her hair around his fingers, hefted the weight of her breasts then set them bobbing in the water. He slid a hand down her belly to toy with her clit. Inexorably, he stroked and circled and brought her to orgasm as she had done for him. She arched into his touch, thrashing until the water sloshed over the edge of the bath. Afterward she collapsed against him with a contented sigh.

He wrapped his arms around her body. The colors on his wet arms looked like fresh ink. Absently, Sarah traced the figure of the angel.

"This is really quite beautiful. Her expression is so serene."

"It's my mother. I mean, the face is hers."

There was a long pause and she felt his chest rising and falling against her back.

"He loved her, I think."

Sarah felt cold despite the hot bath. The tattoo artist was more twisted than she had imagined.

"Or at least he wanted to have her."

The room was so quiet only the faucet's drip and the little splashes they made as they shifted in the water disturbed it.

She stroked his forearm. "Did he ever have her?"

"Did he fuck her? No. I don't think so. ... Maybe."

She stiffened at the word 'fuck.' It sounded so harsh yet so casual when he said it. She wasn't used to hearing profanity and despite everything they'd done together, it shocked her.

She laid her hand on top of the water and brushed her flat palm across the surface. "How did she die?"

He brought his palm up from below the water to press it against hers. "She was sick. She had a bad cold in her chest. Greta tried to fix her, but she died."

"Greta?"

"The woman with the beard. She takes care of people when they're sick."

"Your mother was that sick and no one took her to the doctor?"

He shrugged. "I wasn't there when she died. When she got really bad, he sent me to stay in his trailer. I didn't get to see her again. He buried her wherever we were."

Sarah knew 'he' meant Reed. She'd never heard Tom refer to him by name, only with that distancing pronoun as if Tom were speaking about God--or Satan.

"After my mother died, Greta and Julianne took our trailer and I stayed in the back room of his."

She wondered if Reed had abused him in other ways,

but couldn't bear to ask. If he wanted her to know, Tom would tell her. She laced her fingers through his, allowing him to draw her hand underwater until it disappeared beneath the rippling surface. "Do you still have a headache?" she asked. "I forgot to give you an aspirin powder."

"A little. Not so bad now."

She looked up at him over her shoulder. "My skin's like a prune and the water's getting cold. Shall we get out now?"

She pulled the plug and they rose, dripping, and wrapped themselves in towels. After they were dried and dressed, Sarah gave Tom aspirin powder from the medicine chest.

"Take this then lie down a while? I'll call you when supper's ready."

"The animals. I should—"

"Rest. You need it. There's nothing that can't wait until after dinner." She stood on her toes and kissed him.

Tom's face was haggard and the fact that he didn't argue let her know how exhausted he was. He headed toward John's room, not hers Sarah noted, and she went down to the kitchen where a mound of wilted cabbage lay on the counter. She scraped the shreds into the compost bucket and sliced into a new head to make coleslaw.

She too was drained from the stressful day, but she moved around the kitchen, going through the familiar, homey tasks of slicing bread, peeling potatoes, and breading pork chops. Keeping her hands occupied helped keep her mind off of bigger worries, but she couldn't help dwelling a little on how the townsfolk were going to react to Tom living with her. She hoped the people she considered friends would prove to be true allies.

The kitchen was rich with the smell of baking pork chops and apples when Sarah heard a car coming up the drive. She wiped her hands on her apron and went to the front door, steeling her nerve to face whoever had come to see her. She had no doubt what the subject up for discussion would be.

Grace May cut the engine and climbed out of the Ford with a wave. "Got time to talk?"

Sarah gestured her to the porch swing. "Sit down. Let me guess what you want to talk about."

"Where is he?"

"Upstairs sleeping. The search really wore him out."

"The whole thing is amazing. I didn't believe in that kind of thing, but Mike told me what happened and it seems real. The fact that this guy knew where to dig for Aileen proves it. Unless he buried her there himself, or happened to be there and saw the cave-in, there's no other explanation for it." Grace shook her head. "And you hiding him here all these days. I didn't know you could keep secrets so well. Why didn't you tell me?"

"I didn't see you right away then, when I did, you were with Mike and Andrew so I couldn't talk freely. Besides, I didn't want to break Tom's confidence." Sarah wasn't sure that was all of it. She knew what a gossip Grace could be and hadn't really trusted her to keep such a big secret. And maybe there'd been a certain element of excitement to having a clandestine life that not even her friend knew about.

"So, what's he like? Mike said he's not mentally slow, just quiet, and that he was kept some sort of prisoner at that carnival."

"That's right. He wasn't always locked up, but Reed made him believe he had no place else he could go. Look at him. It's true. That man made him so he couldn't possibly fit in anyplace except a carnival."

Now that Grace had opened her up, the thoughts Sarah had kept to herself all week spilled out. "He kept him from having a normal childhood, didn't teach him anything or allow him to interact with other people." Except in ways she would *not* tell Grace about. "When I discovered him in the barn last week, he barely spoke. Not because he isn't capable, but because he is so unused to talking with people."

Grace rocked the swing gently. "Poor guy. What about his family?"

"His mother was a fortune teller in the carnival and when she died Reed took control of him. Tom was only eight."

"That's awful."

"There's really no place for him to go and he's been very helpful around the farm. It's been good having him here."

Grace stopped rocking and faced her. "But he can't continue to live here. I mean, he's not some stray dog you've taken in. What will people think?"

"I don't care what they think." Sarah heard the petulance in her voice and didn't care about that either. Why should she have to worry about people's opinions? Hadn't she been through enough heartache? Didn't she deserve some happiness?

Grace frowned. "Well, you'd better care. *I* understand that you're simply being kind and helping this poor soul, but it might not look so innocent to others. And, honestly Sarah, you haven't really seen the bad side of the people in this community yet. Some of them can be very narrow-minded and ... harsh."

Sarah remained silent. The steady rasp of cicadas seemed exceptionally loud.

"You should let Tom stay with Mike and me. We could bunk him down in the old tool shed. It's watertight and I could set up a cot for him."

"Thank you, but I'm happy with things the way they are. I have plenty of room here, and like I said, Tom's very helpful in doing odd jobs." She toyed with the unraveling hem of her apron.

"You *have* been lonely. I knew it. You like having someone around." Grace's eyes widened. "Oh my gosh! Are you...? Do you *like* him? I mean, are you interested in him *that* way?"

Sarah stared across the yard at the garden. She could have protested, but she was such a bad liar and Grace knew her too well.

Grace covered her mouth with her hand. "You haven't... Have you?"

"Yes," Sarah said flatly, looking her right in the eyes.

"Sarah!"

"Why not? I'm an adult and it's my business. Besides, aren't you the one who's been encouraging me to start living again?"

"Yes, but not like that!"

"Don't be such a prude," she said lightly, trying to cover her growing fear. Would Grace find her behavior so immoral that she'd lose her friendship?

"I'm not a prude. It's not about the *sex*," Grace whispered the word. "It's who you did it with. How could you? I mean..." Her tone changed from shocked to curious. "How was he? Was it different?"

Sarah bit her lip, ashamed to be gossiping but desperate to share everything she'd been holding inside. "Yes. He's nothing like John. Nothing like him at all."

"Really? What was different? Did he...?" Grace waved a hand as though erasing a chalkboard. "Oh, forget it. I shouldn't be asking this. It's too private. But," her voice lowered, "is he tattooed *everywhere*?"

It was wrong to discuss Tom like this, but she needed to confide in her friend. "He's beautiful, like a stained glass window. And he's really good with his ... mouth."

Grace gasped and giggled. "But isn't it strange? Touching him?"

"Skin is skin, Grace. The tattoos are only on the surface, you know. He's a man." *A sexy, vulnerable, intense, attractive, sweet, gentle and loving man.*

Grace exhaled a long breath and leaned back in the swing. "Heavens to Betsy, you *are* full of surprises. I don't even know what to say."

Sarah leaned back next to her. "Then don't say anything. Really, Grace, there's nothing you and Mike need to do about this. I'm a grown woman and it's my decision. As my friends, all I ask you to do is support me and continue to *be* my friends."

Grace squinted at her. "Have you been careful? The last thing you want is an accidental pregnancy."

Sarah blushed at Grace's bluntness and because she knew her precautions had been questionable. "Pretty careful." Her period was due any day now and she'd soon find out if they'd been careful enough. A flutter of fear stirred in her chest.

"Well, listen. I know Rev. Brighton says abstinence is the only godly way to keep from having babies, but Mike and I use other protection. We aren't ready to start a family quite yet and God created the man who invented condoms, didn't he? So He must want us to use them. If you need some, I'll drop some by since you obviously can't get any at the pharmacy. Ed Reinholdt would spread it around town quicker than you can say jabberwocky."

Sarah impulsively leaned over and hugged her. "Oh Grace, I thought you were going to hate me now or maybe be disappointed in me. Thank you so much for being my friend."

Grace returned the hug. "I won't preach at you, Sarah, but it doesn't mean I agree with what you're doing. And, honey, you must know this is not going to fly with the people around here. You'd better expect some rough weather ahead."

Chapter Ten

Grace's prediction proved right.

After a lull, which included all of that evening, a peaceful night of sleeping entwined together and a bright Sunday morning, the first rumbling of thunder came.

Sarah and Tom took a break from their chores after lunch to sit on the front porch, drinking coffee and discussing plans for the afternoon. An approaching car engine signaled the end of the calm, and a shiny black Hudson pulled into view.

It took Sarah a moment to recognize the minister's car. She'd rarely seen the Rev. Brighton since John's funeral. They had exchanged polite greetings at social occasions, and he always reminded her that everybody missed her at church, but so far he hadn't gone out of his way to try to shepherd her back into the fold.

Today Brighton and his wife Barbara got out of the car and approached with pleasant smiles frozen on their faces. Sarah glanced at Tom, perched on the edge of the porch swing as if ready to disappear inside the house.

"You're going to have to meet people. Might as well

start with the pastor. He and his wife are nice folks."

He nodded and relaxed slightly.

Mrs. Brighton ascended the steps. Her smile was turned on Sarah like a floodlight, but her eyes darted toward Tom. Her wary glance suggested someone afraid of a dog which suddenly bite. "Sarah, how are you? I've been remiss in stopping by to visit you."

Sarah extended a hand, manufacturing her own smile. "Well, I haven't been too social. There always seems to be so much to do around here."

Rev. Brighton clasped her hand in his firm, double handed shake. "I'm afraid I haven't tended to my pastoral duties as well as I might. I apologize for that." He faced Tom, who still stood near the swing. "I thought perhaps your friend here might be able to use the church's aid."

His words put Sarah a little at ease. Maybe the reverend and his wife were actually going to be helpful. Nevertheless, she didn't want to invite them into the house where they might be harder to get rid of if the conversation grew strained She gestured toward the pair of rattan chairs on the other side of the porch.

"Won't you sit and let me get you a cup of coffee? This is Tom, by the way. Tom, this is Rev. and Mrs. Brighton. Rev. Brighton is the pastor of the Methodist church."

Tom nodded silently, but the minister stuck out his hand. After a moment Tom took it. The reverend pumped his hand several times before letting go. "Pleased to meet you, Tom."

After seating their guests, Sarah went to fetch coffee

BONE DEEP

while Tom brought out a couple of the kitchen chairs to place across from the Brightons. Soon the four of them sat in a circle, making polite conversation and sipping coffee to fill in the awkward gaps.

"Little Aileen is fine," the reverend said. "She had to have her leg set in a cast, but other than that she's doing very well and should be home from the hospital by this afternoon. The Brodbecks asked me to pass along their thanks to you. They plan to come and thank you personally soon." He paused then added, "But let me be frank. Rumors are running rampant in the congregation. I wanted to get the story about Tom and the rescue yesterday directly from the source."

Sarah launched into her thumbnail sketch of Tom's life at the carnival, their meeting and his psychic gift, which led to Aileen's discovery.

Mrs. Brighton looked increasingly uncomfortable as the story unfolded, but the minister seemed intrigued. "Do you believe your visions are a gift from God?"

Tom blinked. "I don't know."

"Do you consider yourself a Christian?"

Tom darted a glance at Sarah.

"Reverend, I don't think he received any religious education. I don't think he can answer that."

"Fascinating." Brighton observed Tom like an animal which had gained the power of speech.

Mrs. Brighton set her cup on its saucer with a quiet click. "Sarah, while I admire your Christian charity in offering aid to the needy, I'm concerned about you putting your reputation at risk. Perhaps the church can find a more suitable place for Tom to stay and maybe a menial job somewhere."

"My wife's right. I'm afraid some of the gossips are already having a field day with this. It probably would be best if we hosted him at the parsonage until we can find other accommodations."

Mrs. Brighton looked at her husband sharply, clearly taken aback. "I was thinking of Linus Taylor hosting him for awhile. He's single and lives in his family home alone. A bachelor situation is much more appropriate."

Sarah said smoothly. "Tom is proving very helpful around the farm. I don't mind having him here. I'm sure we don't need to put Mr. Taylor to any trouble, or you either, for that matter."

"Yes, but my dear, this is really not the solution," Mrs. Brighton said. "If you want to hire ... this man to do farm labor, that's one thing, but he cannot continue to live here. It's not seemly."

The reverend nodded. "Your moral character will come under fire, no matter how innocent your intentions."

"I understand that. I'm willing to take the chance." Sarah was proud of her calm, even tone when her body was nearly trembling with rage. The oh-so-polite offer of help came with a heavy anchor of judgment weighing it down.

The Brightons seemed nonplussed and remained silent for a moment, and then the reverend tried a new tack. "Perhaps Tom should make his own decision about his future." He looked at Tom, who had remained mute throughout the conversation. "What *are* your plans for the future? Do you plan to stay around Fairfield or will you be moving on?"

Once more Tom glanced at Sarah, but she couldn't answer for him this time. She'd done far too much speaking on his behalf and wanted to hear how he would answer the questions.

"I want to stay here," he finally said. "I like working on the farm."

"You do understand that your living in this house is very damaging to Mrs. Cassidy's reputation. People won't like it," Brighton said. "Would you be willing to let me find someplace else for you to stay?"

Tom stared his clasped hands a moment then looked back up. "I don't want to make trouble for her. Would it be all right if I stayed in the barn?"

"I'm afraid that won't stop people talking."

Sarah interrupted. "Reverend, I appreciate your concern, but as I said, I'm happy with the arrangement we have here. People who choose to gossip are already doing so. I don't know if moving Tom somewhere else is going to stop them."

Brighton exhaled loudly, his pastoral patience wearing thin. "Well, I can't force you to change your mind, but I'll still talk to Linus Taylor and see if he'd be willing to help out—in case you change your mind."

The Brightons rose to leave at last. The minister shook Tom's hand but his wife avoided touching him. Before Mrs. Brighton walked away, Tom looked at her intently and froze just for a second. Neither of the Brightons noticed, but Sarah saw.

The Hudson's wheels churned up gravel and dust as the car drove away.

Sarah turned to Tom. "Did you see something about Mrs. Brighton?"

He shook his head. "It's her business."

Of course that piqued her curiosity even more, but she dropped the subject and slipped her arms around his waist.

"Don't mind what they said. I don't want you to move out. The kind of people who gossip aren't ones I care about anyway."

He held her with one arm and stroked her hair away from her face, studying her features as though memorizing her. "People can make things hard. If they're angry enough, they could even hurt you. I should go."

She stood on tiptoes and covered his mouth with hers, stopping his words. "If you think I'm doing you some sort of favor letting you live here, you're wrong. I'm being purely selfish. I want you here. I haven't been this happy since before John died and I am not going to lose you."

He gave a little half-smile and hugged her tight, burying his face against her neck.

I will not let you go, she repeated to herself. *I'm finally starting to come alive. There's no way I can go back to being half dead again.*

Chapter Eleven

They spent most of Sunday afternoon in the garden digging up potatoes and removing stripped corn stalks and cabbage stumps. At the end of their work they were filthy, and Sarah suggested another swim in the pond even though the day was chilly. She loaded a picnic hamper, and they walked across the field.

At the pond's edge they both stripped unselfconsciously and swam naked in the cold water. After racing the length of the pond, they circled each other, drawing closer and closer until they floated in the water face to face. Hazel eyes stared into blue, until finally Sarah broke the intense connection and threw her arms around Tom's neck.

He cupped her bottom and pulled her against him. She wrapped her legs around his waist and kissed his wet lips, tasting pond water. His back was smooth and slippery beneath her hands. Cool water lapped her body, sending shivers through her. The moment was delicious and perfect. Only a few weeks ago, Sarah hadn't imagined she'd ever feel such happiness again.

Tom's tongue dipped delicately between her lips. She touched it lightly with her own. Then their mouths fused together hungrily and they didn't pull apart until both were breathless.

Sarah gazed into Tom's eyes, which reflected the sunlight like a prism making a thousand shades of blue. Her heart ached at the strength of her feelings and the words she wanted to say filled her throat and choked her. *I love you.*

She leaned down and kissed him again.

He waded out of the pond, carrying her. After drying off, they spread their towels on the ground. Tom lay on his back and Sarah straddled him, looking down at his face and not even seeing the markings anymore but only the features beneath them. She leaned to kiss him, her pussy brushing against his erection, generating delightful tingles.

A rustling in the bushes across the pond was followed by a titter of suppressed laughter. Sarah's head jerked toward the noise and she threw her arms across her naked chest.

Muffled voices and the patter of running feet came from the stand of trees.

Sarah scrambled off of Tom, grabbed his shirt from the grass and covered herself with it. Tom sat and pulled one of the towels over his groin. But by the time they were covered, the sounds from the woods had faded.

"Damn! Damn, damn, damn." She'd been so stupid and careless to use this pond as if it were a private pool when she knew local kids sometimes came for a swim. She'd thought the day was too cool and that it was too late in the year to expect anyone to be there. She should've known kids would have nothing better to do on a Sunday afternoon.

Sarah kicked the picnic hamper, knocking it over and

spilling ham sandwiches onto the ground. "Damn!" Her stomach twisted in knots. Kids would whisper the story to other kids and eventually an adult would find out. Soon the whole community would know. It would no longer be just a rumor that the Cassidy widow had taken the tattooed man from the carnival as her lover.

Tom crouched to pick up the sandwiches. He righted the basket and looked up at her with anxious eyes. "I'm sorry."

"No. It's all right." She dropped to her knees to help. "I want people to know about us. I do. Just not in this way." She picked up a sandwich and brushed dirt off the waxed paper. "But it'll be all right. People will get used to us being together. They'll have to."

The following afternoon, Grace's Ford pulled into Sarah's driveway again. She was out of the car before Sarah clipped the last clothespin to the flapping sheet on the line.

"Is it true?" Grace shook her head without waiting for an answer. "How could you be so dumb? So careless? The Weiderman boys told all the kids at school what they saw at the swimming hole. Those kids who weren't afraid of having their mouths washed out with soap told their parents and now everybody knows, the whole town, probably the whole county by now!"

Sarah closed her eyes. Less than a day and the gossip had spread through the community like wildfire. She'd expected it, but having her expectations become fact was a hard slap in the face. She had been fooling herself in thinking people would take this affair lightly. And it wouldn't have mattered if she'd been caught with someone as respectable and upright as Andrew Harper. Good Christian people didn't condone extra-marital sex—particularly when their children caught an eyeful.

Tom came out of the barn balancing a ladder on his shoulder. He stopped when he saw Grace, set down the ladder and came over.

"Tom, this is Grace.

Grace cocked her head slightly regarding Tom then held out her hand to shake his. "Hello."

He shook her hand the way the minister had done his yesterday, with a vigorous two-handed pump. He was learning social behavior as he went along, mimicking other people since he had no frame of reference for manners. By watching Sarah, he'd learned how to eat politely. Now apparently he was patterning Rev. Brighton. Tom's resiliency in re-shaping himself after years of living a stunted life was remarkable.

Grace's dimple flashed in her round cheek as Tom gravely shook her hand and Sarah knew he'd won her over.

"All right," Grace said, turning her attention to Sarah. "I'm not here to scold but you'd better know it's going to be like the Antarctic or hell next time you go to town. People are either going to give you the silent treatment or tear into you." She added reassuringly, "Not everyone. There are some who think the whole thing is none of their business."

"But you can count them on one hand, right? And they're both named Cunningham."

Grace shrugged. "Anyway, I can't stay long. I'm

running an errand in Hooperstown but I wanted to let you know what's happening." She patted her purse. "Also I have what we talked about the other day."

"Oh." Sarah looked at Tom, "Could I talk to Grace alone for a moment?"

He bowed his head toward Grace. "Nice to meet you." He offered her a small smile before going to pick up the ladder.

When he was out of earshot, Grace raised her eyebrows at Sarah. "Wow, sweet smile and amazing eyes. I can understand the attraction." She reached in her purse and handed Sarah a small box. "Directions are inside if you've never used them before." Her normally pink cheeks were bright red.

"Thank you." Sarah accepted the condoms, her own face flushing, and put the box in her apron pocket.

After Grace drove away, Tom set the ladder against the eaves at the side of the house where he was going to clean out the gutter and came over to Sarah. "It sounds like there's going to be trouble. I didn't mean to make things so hard for you. I should leave now before it gets worse."

Sarah shook her head. "So people know the truth now. We'll simply have to face up to it and wait for the gossips to get bored talking about it and turn their attention to something new."

She forced confidence into her voice but inside she knew it would not be so easy. The villagers may not come marching in with pitchforks to drive Tom off, or brand her with a scarlet A, but it could be very unpleasant being stared at and ridiculed. Tom had suffered enough of both in his life. She wished she could spare him that.

After a supper of corned beef, new potatoes and cabbage that evening, Sarah served chocolate cake for dessert. Tom's eyes closed in pleasure as he ate a mouthful of dark cake and rich butter frosting.

"I've never had anything like this."

"Never? Then have a second piece." Sarah thought of all the things she could cook or bake for him. In her mind she prepared meals for him for the next fifty years.

When dinner was over, they retired to the living room where Tom worked on his lesson. In addition to slowly reading lines from one of John's childhood books, he could now print all the letters of the alphabet and string some together into simple words. He practiced reading and writing for over an hour then listened to Sarah read aloud from Tom Sawyer.

She was at the pivotal scene where Injun Joe chased the children through the caves when a loud crash came from the front of the house. Sarah bolted from her seat and her heart pounded.

On the floor in the front hall was a brick in the midst of broken glass. Air blew through a jagged hole in the window beside the door. Outside a car engine roared and tires sprayed gravel, but when Sarah pulled the door open, the red taillights were halfway down the road.

She turned on the porch light and stepped outside with Tom right behind her. There was nothing to see in the yard except the deep grooves the tires had cut in her lawn. The damage was done. The message delivered.

Then she noticed a white gleam on the side of the barn. The porch light didn't extend far enough for her to see what it was so she got a flashlight and played the light over the barn. Another message besides the brick had been left for her.

"Freaks Hoar" proclaimed the straggling white letters about the height of a man.

Her jaw tightened as she reined in pure white-hot rage.

"What? What does it say?" Tom was at her side, eyes scanning the letters as he tried to sound them out.

"Nothing. Just stupid, small-minded nonsense. It's nothing." She grasped his hand.

His gaze darted back and forth between her face and the barn. "No. Tell me."

She shook her head. "I don't want to say it. It's a stupid insult, that's all. *And* it's spelled wrong." She tugged on his hand. "Come on. Let's cover the window and clean up the glass."

Sarah crunched across broken shards to get a broom and dustpan. Tom cut a piece of cardboard from a box to temporarily seal the window. They worked silently as they cleaned up.

When Tom was finished, he hefted the brick in his hand, turning it over and over, feeling the texture. "I'm going to check on the animals."

"I'm sure they're fine. Don't go out there. Stay inside." Even though she didn't believe there were any other hooligans lurking around, she didn't want to watch Tom disappear into the dark night.

"I'll be right back." He picked up the flashlight and left without another word.

Sarah stood on the front porch and watched anxiously as he crossed the yard. He opened the door next to those awful, dripping letters and disappeared inside the barn. After a few moments, light came pouring out of the barn door casting in a yellow rectangle on the ground. Sarah wrapped her arms around herself, shivering in the cool air and waited for Tom to reappear.

It seemed to take forever, but finally the light went off and his dark shape emerged from the barn.

"Is everything okay?" she called as he approached.

He stopped on the bottom step and looked up at her. The dark, somber look she knew so well was back in his eyes. "This happened because of me. I'm sorry. I should never have come here."

She reached for his hand, pulling him up the steps and into her arms. She hugged him tight and spoke against his chest. "Don't say that! I told you how I feel. I'm glad you came to me and I'm not afraid of facing these people. We just have to be strong and stand firm against their insults."

His whispered against her hair, "I don't belong here and they know it."

"Yes you do. You do belong here." She took his face in her hands and looked in his eyes. "You belong with me."

She led him inside and up the stairs to her bedroom then took him into her arms and inside her body. She held him until he shook with ecstasy and spent inside her.

Chapter Twelve

The next morning Sarah announced they were going to town. "I'm not going to wait for people to whip themselves into a frenzy gossiping about us. We're going to do the regular shopping errands and we're going to do them together. Let people know we're a couple and that we're not hiding out here."

Tom poked listlessly at his eggs. His plate had been in front of him for five minutes and was still full. Nothing could indicate the level of his distress more. "I don't think that's a good idea."

Sarah tapped her finger against her coffee cup and considered. Perhaps she was being impulsive. Forcing people to acknowledge them might only stir the pot even more. But she thought of those white letters on the side of her red barn made her angry all over again. "We need to buy glass for the window from the hardware store anyway."

Two hours later they pulled up in front of McNulty's and got out. Only a few people were on the sidewalk, but more were behind each shop window. Sarah was aware of eyes watching as she opened the trunk. Tom lifted out the window frame from which he'd removed the broken glass and carried the frame into the hardware store.

Andrew was working. Sarah steeled herself for a disapproving look when he noticed their arrival, but his expression remained neutral. He put down the package of lures he was hanging on a display rack and came over to them.

Sarah faked a smile. "Hi, Andrew. Can you replace the glass in this frame?"

"Sure thing." Andrew took the wood frame from Tom. For a second their gazes met and held, then they both looked away.

"If I do some grocery shopping and a couple of other errands, could I pick it up after?"

"Mm. That's pushing it. I won't be able to get to it before late this afternoon."

"All right. I'll probably check back tomorrow then."

The three of them stood awkwardly silent for a moment. Sarah's arms were folded. Tom stared at the floor with his hands in his pockets. Andrew clutched the frame.

"Have you heard how Aileen is doing?" Sarah asked, although Rev. Brighton had already filled her in.

"All right now. Leg's in a cast, but she's okay." Andrew's eyes slid to Tom. "You saved the kid's life, you know."

Tom's hunched his shoulders, glanced up and mumbled, "You dug her out."

"Well, everybody played a part. I'm just glad she's safe," Sarah said briskly, ready to leave. "Thanks for taking care of that glass. I appreciate it." She moved toward the door and Tom followed.

"Sarah, wait," Andrew said. "Can I talk to you alone for a minute?"

"Um, sure. I guess so." She nodded at Tom.

He flicked a glance at Andrew before walking outside.

After the door had closed behind him, Andrew said, "I just thought you should know, some kids have spread a pretty nasty rumor about seeing you and this guy at the swimming hole." He looked at her searchingly, begging her to deny it.

Her throat constricted as she knew she would hurt him with her words. "I'm afraid it's not a rumor. I'm sorry, Andrew."

"I ... I see." He stared at a shelving unit then back at her. "I thought you said you weren't ready to be ... Never mind." He turned away, clutching her empty window frame like a lifeline. "I'll take care of this window. It'll be ready for you to pick up tomorrow." His tone was ice cold as he walked away from her.

Sarah opened her mouth then closed it. There was nothing she could say or do to make him feel better. It would probably be best if she simply left him alone. Not until she was outside the store did she remember the red paint she'd meant to buy o cover the hate message on the barn, but she couldn't bring herself to go back inside.

Tom waited for her in the Plymouth. A few people lingered on the sidewalk at a discreet distance, pretending to look in store windows, but actually trying to catch a glimpse of him through the windshield.

Sarah strode to the driver's side and got in, glancing at Tom to gauge his level of tension. His hands were clenched into fists in his lap, but his expression was calm.

"Groceries next," she announced cheerfully before he could ask her what Andrew had wanted.

Entering the grocery store, Sarah picked up a shopping basket and headed for the house wares aisle with Tom right beside her. She selected a few necessary items, laundry detergent, sponges, scouring pads, and tried to ignore the silence that had fallen the moment she and Tom entered the store.

Mrs. Davidson's conversation with Esther Blanch halted and the two ladies, as well as several other customers in the store, stared at Tom. Then Mrs. Davidson whispered something to Mrs. Blanch, set down her coffee mug with a thump and came out from behind the counter.

If Andrew had been polite and forgiving, Mrs. Davidson more than made up for it with her burning glare and icy words. "Mrs. Cassidy, can I help you find anything?"

"Yes." Sarah tried to pretend that this was a normal day. She kept her voice friendly and respectful even though she would have loved to punch the old busybody's face upturned nose. "I wondered if you could order more Yardley's soap for me."

Mrs. Davidson folded her arms. "I don't place special orders any more. Ivory's good enough for most of the folks in this town, at least the ones who don't put on airs. Maybe you should drive over to Camden or Hooperstown for it. In fact, I think you should buy all of your groceries there. They might have more of what you need."

Sarah knew the woman couldn't outright refuse to serve her. Or maybe she could. The store belonged to the Davidsons. Sarah decided to pretend she didn't understand the implication. "No. That's all right. I prefer to shop locally. I can live without any special orders," she said pleasantly, taking a package of toilet paper from the shelf.

For a moment the storekeeper looked like she would further the confrontation, but instead Mrs. Davidson gave Tom one last contemptuous stare then sniffed and turned away.

The quiet hum of conversation resumed, but the voices sounded strained and hushed. Sarah smiled at Tom, but he didn't smile back. It was as if someone had turned the lights out in his normally expressive eyes. No one was home. He was closed and shuttered.

When Sarah brought her purchases to the counter, there was none of the usual chatter and gossip. Mrs. Davidson tallied each item and dropped it into a paper sack like it was an affront to have touched something Sarah's hand had touched. "Twenty-four dollars and thirty-eight cents," she snapped.

Sarah took the money from her purse and paid. Tom lifted the two heavy sacks and she held the door while he carried them out. Before the door had closed behind them, the buzz of women's voices grew as loud and angry as a hive of disturbed bees. She caught the words "perversion of nature" and "sinful behavior" and her blood boiled.

The brief encounters at the hardware and grocery had left Sarah feeling emotionally drained. Holding her head high while people stared and judged was much harder than she'd imagined it would be. She thought of Tom's years in a sideshow, constantly whispered about and gazed at. How had he been able to bear it?

It would've been easy to head the Plymouth back to the farm, but Sarah was determined to run all of the errands for which she'd come to town. At the feed and farm supply a few workers came out from the back to watch Tom heft a sack of grain on his shoulder and carry it to the car. In the post office she got the fish eye from postmaster as she mailed a letter to her sister in California.

At the library Agnes Chapman was sitting behind the circulation desk. Sarah braced for her gimlet gaze of censure. But after a quick glance to see who had entered her domain, the old woman turned her attention back to her work. She didn't look at them again as they walked through the quiet stacks making selections. Sarah thought maybe she hadn't been able to see who it was through her thick glasses.

When they brought their books to be checked out, Agnes studied Sarah's library card as usual and stamped each book. Then she looked at Tom and asked, "Would you like to apply for a library card of your own, young man?"

He looked startled to be spoken to. "Um, no thank you."

She pushed the easy reader books across the counter toward him. "Be careful with them. Don't bend the corners and never lay an open book face down. It breaks the spine. Also, wash your hands before reading so you don't dirty the pages."

"Yes, ma'am." He handled the pile of books as if they were sacred.

Agnes nodded approvingly. Before she returned her attention to her file tray she met Sarah's eyes for a moment and nearly smiled.

Sarah was more shocked by Agnes Chapman's unexpected kindness than she'd been by Mrs. Davidson's rudeness. People could be surprising. It gave her hope.

As they walked down the stone steps outside the library, she took Tom's free hand in hers and held it. "See. I think it will be all right."

He looked down into her face, gazing longingly at her lips as if he'd like to kiss her right then and there. She was tempted to lean in and let him, but the eyes of the town were upon them, whether seen or unseen, and today was not the day for a public display of affection.

They crossed the street to where she'd parked the car. The old men who gathered on the benches in front of the courthouse every day to socialize were in their regular spots, but today they were joined by several younger men. Sarah recognized most of the men loitering near her car. There was Aaron Avery, the barber, talking to Wendell McCoy, the Baptist minister, also a couple of men who looked as if they were fresh from the barber's chair. Standing in a different group were a couple of farmers and handyman Dick Roberts, already sipping from his flask mid-morning.

Sarah let go of Tom's hand as they drew closer to the loiterers. The men weren't exactly blocking their way, but Roberts leaned against the trunk of Sarah's car. They'd have to walk around the cluster of men to get into the car.

Avery and Rev. McCoy acted as if they'd just noticed Sarah and Tom, when she was pretty sure they'd been watching them since they left the library.

"Mrs. Cassidy," McCoy thundered in his rich bass voice. He always sounded as if he was preaching from the pulpit. "Could you spare a moment."

"No. Not really. I have some repair work to do at home. Someone broke my window last night." She reached into her purse and got her keys ready.

"That's unfortunate. Young hooligans up to hijinks no doubt."

"Maybe." Sarah sensed Tom beside her, tense as a bowstring.

"Young people sometimes don't know the appropriate way to approach a problem and they lash out in an unacceptable manner," the reverend said. "Counseling sinners is best left to the clergy."

Sarah felt the hair on her neck rise. Under the scrutiny of almost a dozen men, including the oldsters on the benches, she felt surrounded and trapped even though no one had made any overtly threatening moves. "Didn't Jesus say something about letting God do the judging?"

"No one is judging, Mrs. Cassidy."

"Look, let's cut through the crap," Dick Roberts interrupted Rev. McCoy. He pushed off the back of the car and stood on the sidewalk in front of Sarah and Tom. "It's not the fornicating that's the problem so far as I'm concerned. It's that"—he pointed at Tom—"unnatural freak."

"Brodbecks are my neighbors and I'm as glad as anybody their little girl's all right," one of the farmers said. "But that doesn't mean I want this guy living anywhere near me or mine. He doesn't belong here."

Suddenly all of the men were speaking at once, everyone voicing an opinion about extra-marital sex, psychic abilities or tattoos. They couldn't even agree on what to be upset about, but every man there knew that there was something very wrong with Tom, and with Sarah by association.

The men drew closer physically, gathering around the Plymouth, shouting to be heard above each other, and making it impossible for Sarah and Tom to move without bumping into someone.

Then Avery was in Sarah's face, jabbing his finger. "My kid was with the Weiderman boys and saw everything—and I mean everything. It's sick is what it is, when your kid can't go to the local swimming hole without coming across something obscene like that!"

"I apologize for that. It was very bad judgment on my part and—" Sarah's apology was drowned out by the clamoring men.

"Leave her alone." Tom's voice was hoarse as he grabbed Sarah's arm and pushed her partway behind him to protect her. She could just see his profile as he scanned the angry, arguing men surrounding them. He looked like a cornered animal, wild-eyed and ready to claw his way free if need be.

"Slut!" someone yelled.

"It's an abomination," another voice said. "A good man like John Cassidy dies for his country and his widow takes up with some freak."

"God *will* judge, but we must steer the wayward back onto the path of righteousness with words," the minister brayed.

"What I want to know is what other kind of devil powers he has. He's unnatural."

Bodies pressed closer, the ripe stench of sweat and hair pomade nearly choking Sarah. She was jostled against Tom, knocking him into Roberts, who pushed back. In the blink of an eye the ugly mood escalated to physical violence.

Tom dropped the stack of library books and glanced at Sarah to make sure she was safe. As he turned back around, Roberts punched Tom in the jaw, knocking his head to the side. Drunken Roberts lost his balance and fell into Tom, bearing them both down to the sidewalk.

Tom twisted out from under the other man's body and leaped to his feet. Sarah caught a glimpse of his enraged expression, tried to reach out to stop him, but was pushed back by a man in overalls.

Roberts scrambled up and took another swing at Tom. With a wordless cry, Tom charged the handyman, driving a shoulder into his gut and knocking him back against the Plymouth with a hard thud.

More bodies pushed between Sarah and the fighting men. She was roughly shoved to the back of the crowd until all she could see was cotton shirts sweated to men's backs. She could hear the sounds of punches and grunts as she fought to get closer to Tom. It sounded as if more than two were involved in the fight now.

"Stop! Stop it!" She beat against the back of a man in a grimy T-shirt and suspenders. "Move! Let me through."

"For cripes sake, cut it out," one of the bench-sitting old men called.

The sound of flesh hitting flesh was almost drowned out by the shouts of the men. Sarah was horrified. They'd turned from a group of people she knew, to an angry mob and Tom was at their center, maybe being beaten to death. She continued to scream and try to muscle her way between the wall of bodies.

"Hey! What's going on here?" Deputy Phil came barreling up the sidewalk from the direction of the sheriff's office. "Break it up. All of you. What in tarnation are you doing?"

His badge and uniform were enough to part the crowd like the Red Sea. As the men stepped aside, Tom, Dick Roberts and a couple of other men were revealed. Tom lay on his side and one of the men gave a last kick before the deputy pulled him away. "Cut it out before I arrest you all."

Sarah dashed over to Tom and dropped to her knees beside him. He was bleeding from his nose and mouth, his body curled protectively around his stomach. He wheezed for air.

Sarah touched his face. "Are you all right?"

"Yeah," he gasped. He rolled over and pushed up onto all fours.

She glared up at the deputy. "Arrest those men. Dick

Roberts attacked Tom."

Phil looked confused and at a loss. He was equipped to write speeding tickets and citations for minor violations of the law, but defusing a group of angry citizens was not his strength. "Mrs. Cassidy, if I arrest Robert or any of the others, I'll have to arrest your friend too. Look what he's done to them."

For the first time Sarah's eyes strayed from Tom to the rest of the combatants. Besides Roberts there were two other men, all with split lips or bloody noses, all clutching injured body parts. Tom had inflicted plenty of damage before they'd fought him into submission.

"It's all right." Tom staggered to his feet and Sarah wrapped an arm around him to keep him upright.

"Deputy, the situation got out of hand," Rev. McCoy said. "Some of us were merely here to speak to help Mrs. Cassidy see the error of her ways. These fisticuffs are not condoned by all of us here."

"Pompous ass," Roberts muttered.

"But you didn't try to stop it, did you?" Sarah turned her anger on the minister. "You're just as bad as they are."

"Enough, Sarah," Tom muttered. "Leave it be."

At the mention of possible arrests, most of the men had drifted away. Now Phil dispersed the rest of them, clapping his hands as though showing pigeons. "Everybody move on. Break it up."

Still grumbling and arguing, they obeyed, even the self-righteous Rev. McCoy and Aaron Avery, who muttered that if anyone was charged it should be Tom and Sarah for public indecency, doing perverted things where kids could see them.

"If you're not going to arrest anybody, then at least help me collect my books and keys," Sarah snapped at Phil. The books had been trampled and scattered, one of them knocked as far as the courthouse steps. The keys had been kicked near the benches. One of the old timers picked them up and held them out to the deputy.

Phil silently collected the damaged books and keys while Sarah guided Tom toward the car. "I'm sorry about those idiots," he said, setting her books in the back seat.

Tom shook Sarah's helping hands off him and slid into the passenger seat with a pained grunt. "I'm all right."

"Maybe I should take you to the doctor. You might have broken ribs."

"No." He slammed the car door closed.

Sarah stared at the car a moment then turned to Phil. "I'm sorry I yelled at you. I was frightened. I knew people might be rude, but I didn't think they'd get violent." She told him about the previous night's incident.

"Don Beach is on shift tonight. Do you want him to cruise by your place a few times during the night? It might scare away any kids out fooling around."

Sarah was annoyed at his characterization of the vandalism as 'fooling around' but grateful for the offer. "Please. That would make me feel a lot safer."

As she turned to get in the car, he put a hand on her arm. "It'll blow over, Mrs. Cassidy. People gotta have something to make a fuss about. Next month it'll be something new." He gave her an encouraging smile.

"Thanks, Phil."

She slid behind the steering wheel and looked over at Tom, his arms wrapped around his stomach and his face blood-streaked as he stared blindly out the window. "Are you sure I can't take you to the doctor?"

"No!" He sounded as close to angry as she'd ever heard him.

She dropped the subject and started the car.

Silence fell between them, but Sarah was too full of things she wanted to say to keep quiet for long. "I am so sorry about what happened today. I practically forced you to come to town with me when you told me it wasn't a good idea. I guess it will take people time to accept us and I can't force—"

"No," he interrupted, still facing the window. "They never will. They'll always hate someone like me." His voice grew soft. "Men like that preacher are the worst. They like to talk about sin and hell and how filthy you are while they fuck you."

Sarah's felt as if someone had punched the breath out of her. Someone had done that to him. Literally. And she had no idea how to respond. She felt physically sick at his harsh words and desolate tone.

"Not everyone is like that, Tom. Some people will always be small-minded. But I do have friends in this community. I'm sure things will get better in time."

He remained silent the rest of the ride home and when they got there, he refused to let her check out his injuries or clean up his face. He shut himself in the bathroom for a while and came out with the blood washed away and only a swollen nose and the beginnings of a black eye to show he'd been fighting.

Sarah tried to get him to lie down and rest but he said he needed to do something in the barn. He brushed past her when she tried to take his arm. She wanted to slow him down, get him to look at her, talk to her, hug her, but Tom remained aloof.

She watched through the window as he stood in the yard facing the letters on the side of the barn for a full minute. Then he disappeared into the barn. She sighed and turned away, resuming her own chores.

When she stepped out on the front porch fifteen minutes later, he was painting over the white letters with some brown paint he must have found in the barn. The coat of brown couldn't hide the words that she knew were hidden behind it.

Later, when she called Tom for dinner he ate the meal silently and afterward he started to go back outside even though the painting was finished. She imagined he planned to sleep in the barn tonight.

"Don't!" she cried, her heart twisting at the rejection as he opened the door. "I'm sorry I dragged you into town and put you in that situation. What else can I say or do? Talk to me. Please don't be mad at me."

He turned to her, his eyes wide. "I'm not mad. Not at you."

She threw herself against him, wrapping her arms

around him and making him cry out.

"Oh, your poor ribs. I'm sorry for that too. It's all my fault." She hugged him gently and rested her head against his chest.

He slipped his arms around her too and her eyes closed in relief.

"I was thinking," His voice rumbled against her ear. "That I've brought you so much trouble after everything you've done for me. Maybe it's not too late to fix it. If I leave—"

"No!" She pulled back and looked up into his face. It was swollen red around one eye and his nose. Brown flecks of paint marred the blue swirls. "Running away is not going to solve anything."

He stroked her face, his thumb lingering on her lower lip. "If I leave, it will be better."

"Not for me." Tears welled at the corners of her eyes and she blinked them away.

He gathered her close again, kissing the top of her head and rubbing her back. "Don't cry."

It didn't occur to her until later that he never added, "I'll stay."

Chapter Thirteen

They spent a quiet evening with no interruptions. Tom sat on the floor, a pad of paper on his lap and his hand tightly gripping a pencil as he formed letters.

Sarah read more from *Tom Sawyer* then they retired to lay peacefully entwined on her bed. She stroked her hand lightly over his bare torso and even that gentle touch made him wince. She couldn't see the bruises forming under the mottled colors already covering him. She held him close with his head resting on her breast until he slept, then she turned on her side and spooned into the curve of his body. The solid wall of male flesh at her back and his heavy arm slung over her made her feel safe and protected.

When she woke in the morning, he was not in bed. She didn't question the empty place in her bed since Tom almost always rose before her to take care of the stock.

She went downstairs and started making coffee. Then she glanced at the kitchen table and saw a sheet of paper held in place by the salt and pepper shakers.

Her stomach rolled as she picked up the note and read the carefully printed words.

Im sory to go. Love Tom.

Blood pounded in her temples, and for a moment she thought she might pass out. Then she remembered to breathe and inhaled with a gasp. She traced the word love with her finger. He had asked her how to spell it just the other night then practiced writing it over and over.

On the table beneath the note lay the magazine picture of the family vacationing in Virginia Beach. She unfolded and looked at it. Was he telling her Virginia Beach was where he was headed? But no. He wouldn't know where it was or possibly be able to travel so far.

Then it struck her. By leaving the picture behind, he was abandoning his dream of a family. He'd given up hope of leading a 'normal' life with someone like her and laid that fantasy to rest.

Sarah felt as bereft as she had the day the army officer showed up at her door to tell her John was dead. Though she'd known Tom for only a short time, the bond between them ran strong and deep. It wouldn't be unreasonable to call it love.

Did she love him? Could she find him and bring him home? Would he come with her if she found him?

She stood reading and re-reading the six word note as if it might change before setting it down on the table at last. She wiped her hands over her face, clearing her eyes, trying to clear her head.

Okay, this was not a problem. He was walking. How far could he have gotten in a few hours? She would find him, talk to him and make him see reason.

Sarah grabbed her car keys and slammed out the door.

She slowly drove the road toward town, thinking he might have struck off across country in any direction, but trying to convince herself he would stick to the road. When she reached the county road and had to decide whether to turn right or left, she sat at the intersection tapping the wheel and trying to think what Tom would do. Where would a man without a home, family or job prospects go? Where would he imagine his future?

He wouldn't expect to find farm work to do, not after the way he'd been treated yesterday. He might try to head for a city to seek employment, but that seemed equally unlikely. She didn't know how much he knew about the world outside the carnival, how much he'd been taught about life and how things worked.

The insidious idea that had drifting through her consciousness since she read the note became a coherent thought. It was something Tom had said when she asked how the sideshow freaks ended up in the carnival.

People who belong there find their way.

Did he think he belonged there? It was the only life he knew and, like a wounded animal homing to its birthplace, he might return to the carnival and to Reed, his warped father figure.

Reed had said the show was setting up in Hooperstown, but that was over a week ago. Where would they travel next on their route, and how would Tom know how to find them? Hopelessness washed over her. It seemed someone like Tom would be an easy person to track, but the world was so big and he could have gone in any direction.

With a crank of the wheel, Sarah turned the corner and gunned the car toward town. She would talk to Sheriff Ziegler, explain everything that had happened and ask if he might know the carnival's circuit, or if he could contact law enforcement in other districts and have them look out for Tom.

The Plymouth roared down the road, eating up the miles, and Sarah brought it to a halt in front of the sheriff's office with a squeal of tires.

Inside, Deputy Beach was just ending the night shift, reclining in a swivel chair with his feet up on one of the desks and drinking a last cup of coffee.

"Mrs. Cassidy!" He set down his mug and sat up straight. "Is everything okay? I drove past your place a couple of times last night like Phil asked and everything looked all right."

"Can you tell me where the sheriff is?"

"I'm not sure when he's getting in this morning. Is there something I can help with?" The man seemed nervous and uncomfortable. Sarah could only assume he knew what the rest of the town knew about her swimming pool tryst.

She released a shaky breath, and was surprised to find tears prickling her eyes and her throat choked. She cleared it. "I..." What could she say? *My lover is missing can you please help me find him?*

Beach was on his feet in a second, ushering her to the same chair she had waited on the other day. "Sit down. Let me get you a cup of coffee."

With a hot mug between her cold hands Sarah felt a

little better. She took a sip then tried to speak again. "You know about my houseguest?"

He nodded and a flush rose up from his neck. "Uh, yeah."

"He left last night and I'm concerned for his safety. I wondered if you could maybe contact the police in some of the other towns nearby and have them keep an eye out for him. I wondered if the sheriff has any clue about where the carnival was going after Hooperstown. I have a suspicion Tom might have gone there."

"Really? I thought the story was he'd escaped from the place."

"I don't know where else he could go."

"Hm." The deputy dropped his gaze to stare at his shoe. "It's not my place to say but have you considered maybe he don't want to be found? The man left of his own free will, right? Maybe he just ain't comfortable living outside of where he belongs. Maybe he's better off there, and you're better off with him gone."

Sarah clenched her jaw tight, not sure if she felt more like crying or dashing hot coffee into Beach's well-meaning face.

"I'm sorry," he said. "I didn't mean to upset you. If you want to wait, I'll give the sheriff a call at home and see how long he's going to be."

By the time Sheriff Ziegler got there almost an hour later, Sarah was ready to jump up and run screaming around the office. She felt Tom slipping further away with each second wasted.

Ziegler said almost the same thing as Beach. "I could put an APB out on him but are you sure you want me to do that? Might be better to let the man go if that's what he wants. Better for you and for the community."

"If you don't want to help me, fine!" she snapped, standing up. "I'll search for him on my own. But if you might know where Reed's carnival is headed I'd appreciate it."

"No idea. Sorry." He walked her to the door and before she left he repeated, "Best to just let it go, Mrs. Cassidy."

Back on the street, Sarah felt lost. She had animals at home clamoring for food and water by now, and couldn't simply ignore their needs while she drove all over the county. She headed home to tend to them before setting off for Hooperstown.

The next few days were as bleak and hopeless as any Sarah had ever experienced.

In Hooperstown she learned the carnival had been set up for several days the previous week and had then headed south. She followed the highway and at Hastings found they'd been camped at the edge of town until the previous night but were gone by that morning. No one could tell her which direction the carnival had traveled next.

How hard could it be to find something so big, which surely couldn't travel all that fast? But in the next few towns she checked, no carnival had been by in over a year.

Sarah returned home late that evening, wanting to keep on the trail but with no idea where to go next and no one she could question in the dead of night.

Although she had only shared her bed with Tom a few nights, already she missed his warm presence lying beside her. She touched the pillow, still bearing the dent from his head. She hadn't made the bed that morning and, when she'd first walked into the room, with the covers bunched up as they were, for one heart-stopping moment she'd thought Tom was lying there. But the bed was empty and she was alone once more.

The next day she started to second guess her plan, doubting that Tom would really return to a place where he'd been so mistreated. She wondered how he could have managed to find the carnival, let alone travel so far on foot. She limited her search to the Fairfield area, driving to farms in a thirty-mile radius and knocking on door after door asking if anyone had seen the tattooed man. She only received negative answers and strange looks.

By the time she got home that evening she was furious with herself for not sticking with her original idea and tracking the carnival, which was moving further away with every passing day.

As she walked toward the barn to settle the stock for the night, she looked at the neat brown block of paint on the side of the barn obscuring words that she could still faintly see: *Freaks Hoar*.

She considered Tom's tragic life and the cruel people who had made him feel he didn't deserve happiness. She wondered if she could reach him by way of his psychic powers if she concentrated hard enough.

That night as she lay in bed, she beamed a continuous message at him until her head ached, *Come home to me. Please, come home to me.*

By Friday she was completely confused, self-doubting and hearing Deputy Beach's voice in her head saying *Maybe he don't want to be found* over and over. She stayed home, caught up on chores, cried a lot, then drove to Grace and Mike's house to tell them her news and get some friendly sympathy.

Grace was supportive—to a point. "I'm sorry. I know how much this must hurt." Then she added a well-intentioned yet painful dig. "I hate to say it, Sarah, but maybe it's for the best. You had to know there was no future for you with that man."

Sarah bit back the retort that rose to her lips and managed a slight nod, but she made her excuses and left shortly afterward, unable to bear the fact that even her close friend was prejudiced against Tom's uniqueness.

Saturday morning Sarah woke to an icy cold bedroom. She dressed in a shivering hurry and went down to the basement to fire up the furnace. After feeding the livestock and eating a light breakfast, she decided to take another trip to town to see Sheriff Ziegler. When she went into the office, Mrs. Ziegler was on duty, brewing coffee and opening a box of donuts.

She thrust the box at Sarah. "Have one. You look

skinny and pale. Have you been eating?"

Sarah had skipped a number of meals that week, her stomach too anxious to be interested in food. She accepted the donut and a cup of coffee.

"You're here to talk to Jack about that fellow aren't you?" Mrs. Ziegler's mouth was set in a disapproving line. "I'll get him." She went to the sheriff's private office and closed the door behind her. Sarah heard raised voices and after a few moments Sheriff Ziegler emerged, followed by his glaring wife.

"Mrs. Cassidy, how are you?" He shook her hand.

Sarah ignored the pleasantries. "Have you heard anything about Tom? Any rumors? Any sightings at all?"

Ziegler rubbed his hand over his chin and glanced at his wife. Her arms were folded and her toe tapping impatiently.

"Well, see, here's the thing."

"What?" Sarah's nerves tingled.

"The other morning, I didn't tell you everything I know. The truth is Deputy Beach had come across your friend that night walking the road. He pulled over and asked if he wanted a lift somewhere. Tom said he wanted to go back where he came from but didn't know how to get there."

"Let's cut to the chase." Mrs. Ziegler interrupted. "Beach called and woke my lunkhead husband here to discuss it, then he drove Tom clear over to Hastings and handed him over to that carnival man."

"He didn't 'hand him over.' It was Tom's choice," the sheriff protested.

"If you knew a man beat his dog and the dog was too loyal and dumb to stay away, wouldn't you try and save it?" Anna clicked her tongue and turned to Sarah. "My husband is sorry for being an arrogant fool and making decisions in your 'best interest' without consulting you."

Sarah was too excited to be as angry at the sheriff as she should be. "I went to Hastings that day. The carnival had already moved on, but I was probably right behind it. If I'd just kept going I probably would have caught up. Now I don't have any idea how to find it."

Mrs. Ziegler nodded at her husband. "*He* does, and he's ready to take you there right now."

"I don't know what to say." Sarah was as shocked as if Anna had sprouted wings and waved a magic wand. A person never knew from what unexpected corner help and support would come. "Thank you."

"I figured you've had enough heartache already in your life. If he is the man you want, it isn't anybody's right to interfere whether they agree with your choice or not." She glared pointedly at her husband.

Ziegler shrugged. "I'm sorry. I thought I was doing the right thing, especially since it's what the man wanted. I told Beach to give him a ride and to keep quiet about it afterward." He added dryly, "But my wife has helped me see the error of my thinking."

Sarah brushed past the question of blame. "So where is the carnival now?"

"I've been keeping tabs on Reed's operation ever since he left here. Sent out a request to law enforcement in all the nearby counties to keep me informed of his movements and any shady business connected to the carnival. I'd like to find a good reason to shut it down."

Sarah thought the information she had shared about Tom's treatment at Reed's hands should have been more than enough, but she held her tongue.

"Got a call from Twin Rivers yesterday. The carnival has set up near town. It's out of my jurisdiction, of course, but I'd be happy to go with you in case you have any trouble with Reed."

Twin Rivers was a good three-hour drive away. Sarah nodded. "I'd appreciate that."

Mrs. Ziegler smiled smugly. "Good. That's settled then." She gave Sarah a long look. "As for convincing your Tom to come home, remember he's just a man, special mind powers or not, and prone to the know-it-all stubbornness of all men. But if you let him know you won't take no for an answer, I'm sure he'll be back with you before tonight."

Chapter Fourteen

By the time Sarah and Sheriff Ziegler arrived at the field where the carnival was set up, it was mid afternoon. The grounds were crowded with people enjoying the entertainment on a sunny yet cool fall day. The flatbed trailers that transported the rides and the motor homes that housed the workers were laid out in a little village of sorts behind the rides, tents and booths.

Sarah could scarcely breathe, her pulse pounding as if she'd ridden one of the carnival rides. Tom was somewhere in the maze of trailers or perhaps in the sideshow tent right now. Now that she was here, doubts and worries filled her mind. Being here reminded her most people viewed Tom as a novelty. She remembered Grace telling her she had no real future with him, and Deputy Beach advising her to let him go. Was she letting her own willful determination override her common sense? Maybe there *was* no happily ever after for them, and maybe Tom was serious in ending their affair to walk a more familiar path.

Sheriff Ziegler had filled the ride to Twin Rivers with small talk, asking Sarah about her farm, telling anecdotes

Bone Deep

about people they both knew, and never mentioning the reason for their trip. Now he seemed to sense her unease and smiled reassuringly. "Why don't you find Tom and I'll go talk to Reed and keep him out of the way."

Sarah nodded, but after he walked away she felt abandoned. She made her way through the happy crowd. A child begged for just one more quarter for the carousel. A mother scolded her son for filling up on cotton candy. A young woman cooed over the stuffed bear her beau had won for her at a game booth. And Sarah felt utterly alone in the midst of the chattering confusion.

She caught sight of the garish depictions on the canvas of the freak show tent. There was no respect for these people's abnormalities and the idea of her Tom being subjected to scrutiny and ridicule infuriated her. She paid and went inside, not sure of what she would say to him, but knowing that somehow she had to free him from this place.

Inside the stuffy tent the mingled aromas of people, stale popcorn and straw assailed her. Her heart raced, words flying into her mind and out again as she steeled herself to speak to Tom. Would his eyes light up on seeing her? Would he smile? Or would he try to pretend she wasn't there?

There was a small group of people in the tent today and Sarah shuffled along with them, making a slow circuit of the attractions. That was fine with her. She wasn't ready to confront Tom. Approaching slowly gave her time to mentally prepare. She glanced toward where she thought he would be stationed, hoping to catch a glimpse, but a knot of people blocked her view.

She looked at the dwarf, and knew his name now. It was Bernard, the man who'd shown Tom some kindness and friendship over the years. She looked at the bearded woman, Greta, and knew she had healing skills. These were people with hopes, desires, and dreams like everyone. She wished she was invisible so they couldn't see her looking at them.

Then, all of a sudden, there was Tom. He sat on his seat, all of his glorious skin revealed. The people in front of Sarah commented as they studied him as if he were an inanimate object.

"It's obscene!" The woman who spoke sounded shocked and affronted. "That's supposed to be Eve, I think."

"And look what she's grabbing for." Her friend giggled.

"No worse than the bearded lady showing her titties," a man said. "This show's not for kids."

"It's not for anyone. It's immoral," the first woman said, but she gaped at Tom nonetheless. Sarah would've liked to slap her hypocritical, self-rightous pie-hole.

Tom hadn't noticed Sarah yet. He seemed to be lost in his own world, staring across the tent as he had the first night she'd seen him. Her gaze roamed over his now familiar body. She noted the bruising around his eye and nose, visible even through the blue tattoos. And she sucked in her breath at the welts across his ribs where booted feet had left their mark.

The group before her finally moved on and Sarah moved to the front, standing before Tom as if he was a painting in a museum she'd come to admire.

His distant gaze dropped from the point somewhere

above her head as he registered Sarah's presence. His eyes opened wide and he gazed at her—no, *into* her.

For the space of several heartbeats they simply gazed at one another, the special connection Sarah had felt with him since they'd first met sizzled and singed. Then Sarah simply said, "It's time to go home now."

She held out her hand. He stared at it for a moment.

"Come with me," she said softly.

Slowly he rose from his chair and stepped over the rope that divided the displays from the real people. He slipped his hand into hers and his palm was warm, the grip of his fingers strong.

She turned to lead him from the tent, but suddenly he seized her. His arms went around her, hugging her tight, and his mouth pressed into her hair as he whispered, "I can't believe you came for me."

Her hands slipped up his back to hook over his shoulders. She buried her face against his chest, breathing him in, forgetting time and place and simply holding him.

After what could have been a few moments or a hundred years, the surrounding noises began to intrude on her consciousness. The people around them were whispering and staring.

Sarah pulled away from Tom and grabbed his hand again. "Let's get out of here."

"My clothes."

She had forgotten his near nudity. Glancing down at the loincloth covering his groin, she realized it wasn't sufficient, especially in his aroused state. "Put something on.

I'll wait."

He strode away to disappear into a partitioned area in the back.

As the crowd continued to whisper and point, Sarah felt self-conscious and on display. There wasn't a pair of eyes that wasn't watching her, including the carnival folk. As new arrivals entered the tent, people shared the story of the woman who'd embraced the tattooed freak. The crowd grew and Sarah had become the main attraction.

Blood rushed to her cheeks and she willed herself to stop blushing. She wanted to scream at everyone to stop looking at her. She wanted to run away or hide. Instead she straightened her spine, lifted her chin and stared into the distance, pretending she was invisible.

"Girl." A voice caught her attention. The bearded woman beckoned her over.

Up close, the woman was older than Sarah had thought. Her jet black hair was clearly dyed and a network of lines etched her face. Her beard and moustache were scant but real and looked outlandish surrounding pink painted lips.

Greta leaned toward her, puffing alcohol fumes as she spoke. "Be careful. Reed doesn't let go of things he wants. Like Tom's mother for example." She gave Sarah a weighty look.

"What does that mean?"

"I'm only telling you not to underestimate him. If Reed can't have what he wants, then he'll destroy that thing—or person—so no one else can have it."

"You think he...?" She couldn't bring herself to say

BONE DEEP

the words aloud, but it surely sounded as if Greta was suggesting Reed had somehow had a hand in Tom's mother's death.

"This warning is for only for you." Greta nodded toward where Tom had disappeared. "And for him. Take care."

Sarah's gaze darted around the tent searching for something to ground her. This was a bizarre dream. The bearded woman's warning and hints shook her and she didn't know what to do about them. Should she tell the sheriff? But Greta's words were vague. She hadn't outright accused Reed of murder.

Just then Tom reappeared, looking less foreign with most of his body covered in regular clothing. His shining eyes focused on Sarah and when he reached her, he asked quietly, "Are you sure?"

"Very sure." She took both of his hands in hers. "I never wanted you to leave. You know that."

"I thought it would make things easier for you. Better."

"It didn't. Not at all."

As she took his hand to leave the tent, she glanced back at Greta. The woman was smiling.

People stepped aside to let them pass as they made their way to the entrance, but whispered comments swirled around them. Sarah ignored all of them and left the dark confines of the tent for the bright, sunny day outdoors. The sky was clear and blue and the sun a lemon drop. A breeze blew against Sarah's face and it felt like freedom.

She was uncertain whether to wait for the sheriff or

meet him at his car, but then he appeared, coming through the crowd with Art Reed beside him. They were arguing as they approached.

Sarah clasped Tom's hand tighter and she glanced up at him. His eyes were wary and watchful, but unafraid.

She herself was frightened. If what Greta had hinted at was true, then Reed was possibly a murderer. Should she pull Ziegler aside and tell him? But if Greta refused to corroborate the story, then Sarah would only be prolonging Tom's ordeal. It would be best to simply get him out of here as soon as possible and figure out the rest later.

Reed marched up to Tom and planted himself in front of him. "Where the hell do you think you're going? You come begging me to take you back and now you think you can leave again? You don't belong out there. *This* is your home. This is the only place you belong."

"No," Tom said quietly. He dropped his gaze for a moment then brought his face up to stare defiantly at the man. "No!"

Reed's voice went from strident to cajoling. "Do you think she's going to keep you? A few months from now she'll be done with you and then what'll you do? Where will you go? Who will take you in then?"

"Stop it!" Sarah pulled on Tom's arm. "Don't listen to him. Let's go."

Ziegler said, "Reed, the man's made his choice. Leave it be."

"You want him back in your town, sheriff? You think that's not going to make trouble in your happy little community?"

"Don't matter if it does. The man's got rights." Ziegler moved in beside Tom. "Come on."

"Think about what you're doing, boy." Reed called as they walked away. "Think about the woman. You don't want to cause trouble for her."

The sheriff looked back. "Are you making a *threat* against Mrs. Cassidy?"

Reed fell silent.

"Good. I didn't think so." The sheriff ushered Sarah and Tom before him past curious fair-goers, past the ticket seller at the entrance, and across the grassy lot toward the sheriff's cruiser.

Sitting in the back seat on the way to Fairfield, Sarah held Tom's hand. They sat close their arms were pressed together from shoulder to fingers. She would've liked to take him in her arms and hold him again, but there'd be plenty of time for that soon enough. Joy swelled in her at the knowledge.

The sheriff tuned the radio to country western music and turned up the volume to give his passengers some privacy.

Sarah noticed Tom's feet were bare. She nodded at them. "He took your shoes?"

Tom flexed his toes. "He didn't need to. I wasn't going to leave."

She wanted to ask why he'd thought going back to that horrible man was his only option, but she already knew the reasons.

"Don't ever leave me again. I won't take your shoes to keep you with me, but I *will* be very angry if you ever disappear like that again." She looked into his eyes to make sure he understood her. "You really hurt me."

He frowned. "I'm sorry. I was just trying to make things better."

"I know. But the two of us apart never going to be the better option. Understand?"

Tom looked at her and one of those slow, sweet smiles curved his mouth. "I do."

Chapter Fifteen

At the sheriff's office, Sarah thanked Ziegler again for helping them and he apologized once more for withholding what he knew.

As she drove home, the enormity of the commitment she'd just made came crashing in on her. By claiming Tom today, she had promised him a life together. And she did want him in her life. She believed what she felt for him was love, but it was so permanent. The idea of a union with someone so different was scary. Eventually she'd introduce Tom to her parents and her sister. Knowing she'd have to explain her choice and fight other peoples' resistance to it for the rest of her life was daunting.

But then she looked at Tom and all her fears melted away. He regarded her with those fathomless blue eyes she would never get tired of looking into.

"Thank you for coming for me."

She teased, "Thank you for being so easy to find."

She pulled the car into the driveway and they walked up the steps to the house. On the porch Tom pulled her against him and gave her a lingering kiss.

She reveled in the feeling of his warm body, his strong arms and his mouth softly exploring hers. She lost all sense of time as he kissed her. At last she pulled away to ask if he was hungry.

Tom was breathing hard and his sky blue eyes had turned to midnight desire. "Later. This first." He lifted her to set her on the porch rail. Her skirt hiked up as she wrapped her legs around his hips. He cradled the back of her skull and continued to kiss her with the fervor of a drowning man gasping for air.

Sarah tugged his shirt impatiently from his pants so she could slide her hands up the silken skin of his back. His muscles flexed beneath her palms and she shivered at the sensation of so much hard, healthy male in her arms. The bulge of his erection pressed against her crotch. She was ready for them both to strip off their clothes and come together right there on the porch. The bed was too far away.

Millie began bawling steadily and loudly, begging for attention.

Tom pulled away reluctantly and regarded her with a heavy-lidded gaze. "I'll tend to the animals."

"We'll finish this later," Sarah whispered.

His hands bracketed her waist and he lifted her down Sarah tore herself away from the temptation of one last kiss ... and one more ... and one more. She hurried inside and quickly assembled a dinner of leftovers.

After setting the table, she poured glasses of lemonade and waited for Tom to come in. But he was taking too long and she was too anxious to see him. She grabbed one of the glasses and walked out to the barn.

The orange light of early evening cast the scene before her in a dreamy glow. Tom was currying Edison, one hand resting on the horse's flank and the other brushing down his leg. Motes of dust and chaff from the hay were suspended in the air, settling on Tom's shirtless body like flecks of gold. In that rich light he looked like a stained glass window. The sweet scent of fresh hay filled the air.

Tom caught sight of her and straightened. Sarah offered the glass of lemonade and he swallowed it down. The muscles of his throat rippled and droplets of condensation from the glass fell onto his chest to roll down the plane of his chest.

Sarah swallowed too. Her body tingled and throbbed in all sorts of places. If she didn't touch him soon, she would explode into a thousand fragments or melt into a wet puddle of need right there on the barn floor. She reached for the top button of her blouse.

Tom finished his drink, wiped the back of his hand across his mouth then saw her unbuttoning her blouse and froze. She pulled the garment off and tossed it aside, unzipped her skirt and let it drop, unfastened her bra and tossed it playfully at Tom.

He let out a low-pitched, growl as he caught it, put it to his nose and breathed in her scent. Then he dropped both bra and glass on the floor. The glass hit with a clunk and rolled a few feet.

Tom stalked toward her like a wolfish predator. Sarah darted away with a laugh and climbed up the ladder to the loft.

He was right on her heels all the way and, the moment they reached the loft, he grabbed her. He attacked her mouth, lips mashed against hers, tongue plunging inside to claim her.

A window at the far end of the loft let in enough light for her to see Tom as he released her and dropped to his knees before her. He slid her underpants down, then gazed reverently at her naked body. Sunset had turned the light a beautiful rose color which bathed both of them in soft hues.

Tom reached up to stroke his hands very slowly from her breasts all the way down her torso. The light, lingering touch was torture. She shivered like an uneasy mare beneath his gentle touch which left trails of heat in its wake.

He nudged her thighs apart and separated her folds with delicate fingers. He leaned closer. The warmth of his breath lifted her brown curls and teased her sensitive bud. When Tom touched it with the tip of his tongue, electricity sizzled at the point of contact. Watching him perform such an intimate act sent alternating waves of exhilaration and embarrassment through her. She embraced the pleasure he gave but a lifetime of modesty made her blush to see the flash of his tongue against her sex.

Then Tom sat back and simply gazed at her sex, examining the glistening folds. He ran a finger between them, dipped it inside of her then brought it to his mouth and tasted her.

She moaned and her entire body clenched at the erotic sight.

You're so beautiful," he murmured, glancing up at her.

She smiled and reached to caress his adoring face. He

offered such pure devotion it was almost frightening. Did she deserve his worship? Could she give him the same level of powerful love?

Tom pressed his mouth to her clit again, kissing and licking it then moving between her labia. His tongue delved inside her and he lapped her juices. He gripped her hips, holding her steady, while he worked her to a frenzy with his talented tongue.

Sarah whimpered and closed her eyes, pushing her hips forward, offering herself to his mouth. Her legs were trembling and if he hadn't held her upright, she might have collapsed.

"Oh, God," she cried, grasping his head and rocking against him. "Oh, God!" The coiling spring of her orgasm rose from the point of contact and spiraled through her. Nerve endings fired until her body was a live wire, sparking and dangerous to touch. She jerked and wailed as she came.

Tom caught her as her knees buckled and lowered her to the hay, soft, yet prickling her backside. He lay beside her, stroking her stomach and breasts. When she finally opened her eyes and looked up at him, he was smiling a trifle smugly.

"Good?" he asked.

"Yes. Very. And you know it."

He kissed her lips and she tasted her own musky flavor. He scrambled up to quickly strip off the rest of his clothes. Rather than lay over her, he reclined on his back, arms crossed behind his head, cock thrusting upward. It was twitching, waiting for her, the black barbed wire encircling the shaft a stark contrast to the rosy skin beneath. Tom looked at her expectantly and Sarah understood she was to assume the position of power this time.

She straddled his hips, a knee on either side and let her pussy brush against the head of his cock lightly. He groaned and his eyes closed as she teased him with the barest touches of her body. He took his hands from behind his head and reached for her, holding her waist and seating her firmly on his cock. As he slid into her heat and wetness, he gave a satisfied grunt.

Sarah sat atop him, moving her hips slightly, feeling his thickness filling her to satisfaction. She smoothed her hands over his chest and the chained heart tattooed there. It moved with his breathing as if it were beating.

She lifted off of him, releasing him from her heat, then plunged down onto him again. It was exciting to watch his cock emerge glistening then disappear inside her. Up and down, slow and easy she rode him. The residual sparkles from her climax started to coalesce. She closed her eyes and writhed against him nearly losing herself right then.

"Sarah," Tom's soft call brought her back from the edge.

She opened her eyes to look at him.

"Stay with me now."

She nodded, understanding his request. Pleasure for its own sake was good, but sharing it with a beloved partner made it even better. Greater.

He pulled her down to him. Her breasts bumped against his chest as she moved. Her long hair fell forward from her face to either side of his. Within the intimacy of that curtain, she locked gazes with him.

They barely moved, thrusting slow and easy, the sound of their breath and their heartbeats filling the silence between them. Sweat beaded on Tom's forehead and he groaned as he thrust even deeper. His cock hit a spot deep inside that made Sarah cry out, but she didn't break the visual connection between them.

His blue gaze seemed to be wordlessly telling her things. Something intangible floated just beyond her comprehension. If she could understand that, she could unlock all the secrets he held inside. She might even be able to see inside his mind as he had sometimes seen into hers.

The sense of powerful connection grew and grew. Her emotions bloomed and expanded like a garden suddenly springing to vivid color. Tom gripped her hips and pushed up into her. His body contracted with the force of the thrust and his eyes closed as ecstasy overcame him.

Sarah felt the wave swelling inside her burst at almost the same moment. Those amazing sparkles of electricity exploded like fireworks. The intangible knowledge just at her fingertips vanished as the power of the orgasm seized and shook her.

Afterward, she collapsed on Tom panting and fused to his body by a skim of sweat. She brushed her tangled hair back and nuzzled into the crook of his neck. A flick of her tongue gave her a taste of salt and Tom's essence.

He held her and stroked her hair, his heart pounding beneath her ear.

Hay pricked Sarah everywhere. Bits of chaff stuck to

her damp skin and her nose tickled until she had to sneeze. Sex in a hayloft might not be as comfortable as making love in her nice, soft bed, but it was exciting.

She snuggled against Tom, grateful to have him back and ready to face any obstacles to their happiness.

"You won't leave again, no matter how difficult things might get for us," she said.

"Never again," he promised.

Chapter Sixteen

The next afternoon the Brodbecks stopped by to thank Tom for saving their daughter. Glenn still seemed uncomfortable around Tom and his handshake was stiffly formal, but Betty's thanks were warm and genuine. She took Tom's hand between both of hers.

"'Thank you' isn't enough. I don't have words to express how grateful I am to you for saving Aileen."

Tom shifted uneasily, not meeting her eyes. He looked like he wanted to snatch his hand away. "I'm sorry it took me so long to find her," he muttered, casting a glance a the girl.

Aileen, leaning on crutches with her leg in a cast stared at Tom curiously.

"How's your leg?" Sarah asked.

"Hurts, but it's my own fault. I feel like an idiot. It was dumb to go in there, especially when nobody knew where I was at." She hobbled forward and offered her hand to Tom. "Thank you for finding me. I ... This sounds weird but I heard a voice inside my head telling me help was coming. It kept repeating it over and over. It was *your* voice. I know it was." She shook his hand then quickly dropped it and stepped back.

Tom smiled slightly, crossed his arms with his hands tucked inside. "Glad you're okay."

The Brodbecks only stayed a few minutes. While Glenn was helping Aileen get into the car, Betty pulled Sarah aside.

"I've heard all the gossip about you and him." She nodded toward Tom, who stood on the porch, leaning against the railing. "And I want you to know it doesn't matter to me. That man saved my little girl and I'll be grateful to him for the rest of my life. We're having a barbecue for family and friends a week from Saturday. You're both welcome to come."

"Thank you." Sarah choked up at the unexpected kindness of the invitation.

Betty went on, "There's something you might think about though. Some people are upset because Tom's so odd looking, others because they think he's got devil powers, but almost all of them are upset by the idea of you two living in sin. If you got married, you could solve some of your problems. I'm sure I'm out of line to say so, but that's my opinion."

"Oh," Sarah said, taken aback by Betty's bluntness. "I'll consider that."

She watched the Brodbecks drive away. *Married*, her mind repeated, as she looked at Tom standing on her front porch watching the curl of dust disappear behind the vehicle. She'd known this man barely two weeks. The idea was crazy. These things were supposed to follow a certain pattern. You dated, got engaged and eventually married. But her relationship with Tom was completely unorthodox, and they'd already made each other an informal promise to be together.

Tom smiled at her, teeth flashing against the blue swirls that decorated his face. She smiled back at him. They could share a bed for twenty years and he might never think to ask her to marry him. Tom didn't follow the usual patterns. If marriage was what she wanted, then she'd have to be the one to propose to him.

Over the next few days, they resumed the routine they'd created for themselves. Their life consisted of chores, lovemaking, meals, lovemaking, reading lessons and more lovemaking. Sarah hadn't been so happy in years. If the weight of community disapproval wasn't hanging over their heads, she would have been perfectly content.

"The baby plays with the dog." Tom's reading voice was slow but confident as he deciphered the words then stopped to examine the accompanying picture. "The dog chases the ball."

He traced a finger over the picture and repeated under his breath, "Baby."

Sarah looked over his shoulder at the colorful illustration of a chubby baby and pudgy puppy with a bright red rubber ball. She thought about the Samuels' litter of pups and wondered if she should get one. It might be nice to have a dog around the place again. Then her eyes drifted to the baby and her heart skipped a beat. She started counting days.

Her period was late, about a week late, which wasn't that much and normally wouldn't have given her any pause. Tonight it started her panicking. She looked at Tom, sounding out the next sentence, and thought about all the times they'd used the condoms Grace had provided ... and all the times they hadn't.

It was too soon to start worrying, too late *not* to worry, but Sarah tried to put the idea from her mind for now.

Tom finished his lesson and she read their chapter of Twain before they went upstairs to bed. When Tom reached for her, she told him she wasn't in the mood. For the first time since she'd brought him home they fell asleep without making love first.

Sarah was deeply asleep when the shock of cold air on her skin woke her. Tom had thrown the covers back and was jumping out of bed.

"What?" she asked groggily.

"Fire. The barn." He thrust his legs into his jeans and ran for the door.

Sarah was still trying to process his words. "What?"

"The barn's on fire." He was out the door and pounding down the stairs before she could move.

Instantly awake, Sarah got up and pulled on some clothes. She pelted down the stairs, hit the switch for the porch lights and slammed out the front door. The black silhouette of the barn against the midnight blue sky showed no sign of smoke or glow of fire but she could hear Edison's frightened whinny and Millie's bawling.

Tom was already halfway across the yard.

Sarah started to race after him. She took two steps across the porch when strong arms seized her and pulled her hard against a man's body. Her attacker pinned to her arms to her sides and a sharp blade pressed into her neck. Sarah sucked in her breath and her pulse skyrocketed to a new level of frenzied panic.

"Tom!" a voice roared next to her ear.

Across the yard, Tom halted.

"Come here. Or I'll cut her throat."

Tom turned and slowly walked toward them. Behind him, an orange glow now showed through the barn windows.

Tom reached the edge of the porch and stared up at Sarah and the man holding her hostage. She couldn't read his expression, but shock best described it.

"Stop right there. Down on your knees. Hands behind your head."

Sarah smelled whiskey on the man's breath and the rancid stink of his sweat as he held her tight in his powerful grip. She would have tried to wiggle away, but the cold metal pressed into her throat held her still. She heard a strangled whimpering and realized it was herself.

The man took a step forward dragging Sarah with him. He stood on the edge of the porch just above the top step.

"I made you, you pathetic freak. You belong to me. If you'd stayed where you belong, none of this would have happened. Look at the trouble you've caused this woman."

"Let her go. I'll go back with you." Tom knelt with his hands clasped behind his head, his gaze dropped submissively toward the ground. "I'm sorry."

"Now you're sorry? Too late," Reed slurred. "Look up. I want you to see what you've done."

Between one breath and the next Sarah felt the knife leave her throat and a burning sensation across her chest, then the blade returned to her throat. She glanced down to find a slice in her cotton shirt with a thin line of darkness welling out of it. She thought the cut on her breast should hurt more than it did and suspected it would eventually.

"If you move, if you try anything, I'll cut her again. And again. Do you believe me?"

"Yes," Tom whispered.

Sarah felt dreamlike, observing but not feeling what was happening to her. Little details caught her attention, like the whites of Tom's eyes reflecting the moonlight and Edison's screams becoming increasingly frantic. She could smell smoke now.

Reed continued. "You know I'll kill her if you don't obey me?"

"Yes."

"Good. Here's what I want you to do. Stand up, take down your pants and show me your prick."

Tom rose and obeyed. His flaccid penis lay small between his legs.

"Did it give you pleasure?" Reed whispered in Sarah's ear, sending a wave of revulsion through her. "Or did it scratch? You know I wrapped it in barbed wire for a reason." He called out to Tom, "To remind you that nothing but pain lies there. The cock twists you up with desire, makes you want what you can't have. Even leads to killing sometimes."

He reached down and cupped Sarah's crotch. "This is what calls you, Tom, but your cock is what drives you to it. I should have castrated you as a child and spared you the pain."

It was then Sarah realized she and Tom weren't going to make it through this. Not only was Reed insane, but logically he couldn't let them go after doing this. He would kill her and without the threat of injury to Sarah to control Tom, Reed would have to kill him too.

"Zip it up," Reed snapped, sounding suddenly sober. "Then pick up that gas can and pour it around the house. Wet the siding."

Tom moved to obey, while smoke billowed out around the doorframe of the barn. Edison still screamed and thumped his hooves against his stall.

As Reed watched Tom pick up the can, he relaxed the knife's pressure against Sarah's neck. Forgetting that he had a live woman in his arms, he dropped the blade a little and relaxed his hold on her. Sarah seized the momentary lapse to twist away from him. She felt a sting as the blade nicked her neck, but she was free. She grabbed Reed's wrist with all her strength and dug her nails into it, shaking it until the knife flew from his grasp. It arched through the air and fell into the darkness.

Sarah spun away from Reed and stumbled down the steps. Tom noticed her movement, dropped the gas can and came running.

Reed lunged down the stairs after Sarah, reaching for her arm, but she dodged away. Howling in rage, Tom charged Reed and tackled him back onto the porch floor.

Sarah tripped on the bottom step and fell to her knees. She glanced back at the two men.

Tom crouched on top of Reed, who was sprawled beneath him. He lifted the man's head and slammed it against the floor. Reed threw Tom off of him and into the railing with a crash of splintered wood, then he scrambled across the porch to grab Tom's shirtfront and drive a fist into his face.

Sarah crawled across the ground searching in the dark for the knife which she thought had landed in the chrysanthemums. A metallic glint caught her eye and she scooped the blade up from the ground. She hesitated, torn between helping Tom and saving the animals from the fire.

But Tom seemed to be doing fine in the fight. He was back on top and pummeling Reed. Sarah ran for the burning barn. Her feet pounded over the ground and she seized the handle of the sliding door. In the seconds before she slid it open, she realized the animals had fallen silent.

When she opened the heavy door, flames fueled by fresh oxygen shot out at her. She raised her arms to protect her head and stumbled backward. Heat blistered her skin. She backed up further, searching for an opening in the wall of fire, but there was none.

She ran to the side entrance. Smoke rolled from under the crack of the door and she could feel heat through the wood. She grasped the handle and singed her hand. Afraid to open the door and face another flare-out, Sarah searched for something to smash the door inward. A large boulder lay nearby. She heaved it up, wrenching her back, and hurled it at the wood door. The heavy stone crashed through the weakened wood and again flames shot out. There was no way for her to enter there.

BONE DEEP

Sarah raced around the barn to the last available door, the one leading into the corral. She vaulted over the fence and ran to the third entrance where the wood seemed warm but not scorching hot. She turned the handle and kicked the door inward. There were no flames but clouds of smoke billowed out. She lifted her shirt over her nose and mouth, eyes tearing from the acrid smoke, and ran into the building.

Darkness engulfed her. Thick smoke obscured everything. Her eyes stung, and her chest ached from holding her breath. She blinked and tried to focus. Flames burned to the left and right of her. Straight ahead was a wall of fire ... right where the animals' stalls should be. It was too late to save Edison or Millie.

Sarah ran out of the building and inhaled a lung full of fresh air to replace the smoke that burned her lungs. The smell of burned fur and charred flesh mingled with the smoke, and she ached at the loss of her beloved animals. She moaned as she gazed at the blazing barn.

But there was no time to mourn now, as she raced back around the building to go to Tom's aid. She still had the knife Reed had dropped, and if necessary, she was willing to stab him with it.

It turned out her help wasn't needed.

The men were in the yard, locked in a lethal embrace, brutally punching each other. As she drew near, Tom kneed Reed in the stomach, doubling him over. Then he knocked the carnival man to the ground and straddled him. Tom held him down by the shoulder and drove a fist into his face over and over. His blows landed like a hammer, striking without pause.

Tom emitted a loud grunt with each punch and he kept pulverizing Reed's face long after the man had stopped moving.

Sarah stood back and watched in morbid fascination. She should stop Tom, pull him off before he killed Reed, but a primitive part of her relished every blow and hoped Tom *would* kill him.

It took the sound of an approaching car and the glare of headlights flooding the yard to shake her free from her detached observation. "Tom, stop. You'll kill him." She moved closer and grabbed Tom's arm the next time he raised it. It was like trying to hold back a steel piston. He tore free and once more slammed his fist into Reed's face, the impact of flesh on flesh making a squelching sound.

"Stop now," she said again.

Tom stopped. Kneeling over his former guardian, he heaved deep, hoarse breaths and stared into the wrecked face.

After a moment he looked up at her. "Are you all right?" Tom rose and stepped over Reed's body to touch the front of Sarah's shirt with one bloody hand. "He cut you."

Charlie Burkett climbed out of his pickup and ran toward them. "Fire engine's on the way!" He looked at the man on the ground. "Jehoshaphat! Who is that? What happened?"

"Arthur Reed. He set the barn on fire and held a knife on me," Sarah said.

Charlie looked at the conflagration. "You didn't get the livestock out?"

"No. I couldn't."

BONE DEEP

"Cripes." He looked from Reed's mangled face to Tom, whose arm was wrapped around Sarah's shoulders, then back to the burning barn. "It's too late to put it out with buckets. All we can do is wait for the fire truck to get here."

The three of them stared at the leaping flames that engulfed the lower part of the barn. They could feel the searing heat even from this distance.

"I woke up when Arnie started barking and whining." Charlie said. "Went to shut him up and saw the light over here. I thought maybe it was a grass fire so I had Mary call the fire department before I came over."

"We should wet the area around the barn." Tom pointed to the licks of flame that were starting to crawl across the grass.

They gathered buckets from the house and Sarah worked the old hand pump in the yard while the men carried pails of water to douse the fire fanning rapidly across the yard. As sparks and embers rained around her, she pumped until her arms ached. When at last she heard the wail of the fire engine, she thought she'd never heard so blessed a sound.

The rest of the evening was a blur. Sarah remembered the flashing red lights of the fire engine and more neighbors arriving to see if they could help. It appeared one wall of the barn might collapse out onto the yard. The firefighters fought it with the spray from their hoses and finally it toppled inward with a crash. The shower of sparks shot high into the sky.

Sheriff Ziegler arrived and questioned both Sarah and Tom. She repeated what she'd told Charlie. "He set the barn on fire and held a knife on me." And Tom gave the same brief response. The sheriff took the knife as evidence, looked at the savagely beaten, barely breathing man on the ground and wrote something in his notebook.

"All right then. Seems pretty cut and dried to me," he said.

An ambulance arrived to transport Reed to the emergency room. The driver wanted to take Sarah too. "You should have that cut stitched and those burns on your hands treated."

"They're not bad, only a little singed. I don't want to go to the hospital. I have a first aid kit here." She stood firm, clinging to Tom's hand.

The ambulance driver shook his head, but closed the door of the van and drove off, lights flashing.

Mary Burkett and Edna Peterson ushered Sarah indoors to tend to her injuries. Edna brewed tea, while Mary washed and sealed the cut with butterfly bandages then rubbed ointment onto Sarah's reddened, blistered skin. Mary also tended Tom's injuries, rinsing blood off his face and hands, packing his swollen knuckles in ice, bandaging a cut on his forehead and giving him another bag of ice to hold against his swelling eye socket.

The sky had turned the gray-pink of dawn before the firemen were satisfied the last of the smoldering embers was out. They finally drove away, leaving charred ruins behind. The stench hung in the air in an invisible, choking cloud.

Tom wrapped an arm around Sarah's waist as she swayed with exhaustion in the middle of the muddy, soot-covered yard. Some of the neighbors stopped on their way to

BONE DEEP

their cars to offer Sarah condolences on her loss and promises of assistance in rebuilding.

The Petersons tried to ignore Tom's presence at her side. The Burketts acknowledged him, and Charlie even shook his hand. People's reactions to Tom were as varied as their personalities. Some didn't even stop to say goodbye, simply drifted away to their cars and pickups now that the show was over.

When the last person had left, only the sheriff remained. "I may need to ask more questions in the next few days, especially if Reed doesn't survive. The man wasn't looking too good when they took him away. Don't worry though. I'm sure it will be clear to any court this was a case of self-defense. If ever a man deserved a beating it's that fellow."

After the sheriff's cruiser drove off, Sarah and Tom were finally left alone to face the smoking destruction of the barn.

"Are you all right?" Tom asked. "Why don't you have a bath and lie down?"

"What are you going to do?"

"Bury them." He nodded at the pile of rubble.

"You don't have to do that. You should rest too."

"I want to take care of it. I need to do something to make up for..." His hands clenched at his sides and he stared at the ground. "I'm sorry for making all of this happen. Reed was right. I should have stayed away from you. I've brought you nothing but trouble."

Sarah grabbed his shoulders and forced him to look into her eyes. "No! Forget everything that man ever said. You did nothing wrong. Not ever. *He* made this happen. I don't know how many more ways I can tell you. I'm happy you came here. You've"—she hesitated over the melodramatic words, but they were the truth and he needed to hear them—"brought my heart to life again."

She took his hands, lifted them to her mouth and kissed the back of each one.

"We'll take care of burying what's left of Edison and Millie later. Right now I have something more important for you to do. I want you to come inside with me. I *need* you to hold me."

His eyes were glistening as he nodded.

They bathed together in a steaming tub of water.

Tom traced the slice across Sarah's chest with a finger then leaned in to place a suturing row of kisses along it. She removed the bandages from his hands and carefully washed his swollen knuckles and battered face.

They gently kissed and touched everywhere, reassuring each other that they were safe, and afterward they lay down to rest while the sun marked the passing of another day.

Chapter Seventeen

"Are you ready for this?" Sarah asked.

She and Tom sat in the parked Plymouth watching the people milling around the picnic tables, the grill and horseshoe pitch in the Brodbecks' yard. It was a fine October day, probably the last chance for an outdoor event, and a large portion of the community had turned out for it.

Tom nodded, but Sarah could see the tension in his face.

They got out of the car and walked toward Betty Brodbeck, who was cutting cake at the dessert table. At least there was one friendly face to welcome them. Betty laid down her knife, embraced Sarah and took Tom's hand. "I'm so glad you could come."

"Thank you for inviting us." Sarah was grateful to her for much more than the invitation.

Betty lowered her voice. "The best way to get people to stop gossiping is to let them get to know Tom. I know it's kind of like being on trial but if you're going to stay around here, you have to do it." She squeezed his hand. "So why don't you grab yourself a bottle of pop from the wash tub and

I'll introduce you around."

Sarah watched Betty lead Tom from group to group. Clutching a bottle of Orange Crush dripping with melted ice, Tom stuck out his hand to one person after another. Betty was a hard-headed woman and no one dared cross her by refusing to greet Tom. In thirty minutes she went farther toward encouraging Tom's acceptance into the community than Sarah could have in months. But then she herself was still considered an outsider from Chicago.

Betty could enforce their politeness for today, but deep-seated prejudices would not be so easily abandoned. And how much ground would be lost when the judgmental townsfolk learned Sarah was pregnant?

She'd driven to the doctor in Camden the previous Friday to take the test and gotten the results by mail yesterday. It had been a week of wondering, worrying and keeping her anxious secret from Tom. She knew he'd sensed her tension all week. He'd sometimes watched her with a worried frown. But she hadn't wanted to say anything until she knew the results.

When she received the envelope from the doctor's office, she had closed herself in the bathroom with it. She read the announcement that her life was about to change over and over until the words blurred in front of her eyes.

Last night hadn't felt like the right time to tell Tom. He was anxious enough about attending the gathering at the Brodbecks' house and there was no point in adding to his worries. She would tell him soon, but for now the news belonged to her alone. The idea of a child growing inside her

BONE DEEP

filled her with both excitement and dread. Her feelings were so conflicted she couldn't begin to sort them out. The only thing she knew with absolute certainty was that when she told Tom, she mustn't reveal any reservations. He already considered himself unworthy of her. She certainly didn't want him to sense that she feared having his child. But, to be honest, she did.

Sarah watched Betty introduce Tom to stiff-necked Esther and Carl Blanch, who barely nodded before turning away. Together she and Tom were already crossing one hurdle, gaining grudging acceptance in this community. The idea of having a child who would always have to fight bigotry was frightening. Sarah pictured a day, six or seven years in the future, when her little boy or girl would come home crying because the other kids teased about being the freak's bastard. Her heart ached for the persecution her child might suffer.

At least the bastard part could be changed. They could be married. She was sure Tom would agree if that was what she wanted.

She remembered her first wedding, herself in a white, satin dress gliding down the aisle toward a smiling John at the front of the church. Replacing John with Tom in her mental picture simply didn't work. The idea of a traditional wedding was impossible. Maybe a justice of the peace would do.

She thought about the commitment of 'forever' between two people who had yet to say the words "I love you" to one another.

"Hi," Andrew Harper's voice startled her from her musing.

"Oh, hi Andrew." Sarah smiled weakly. She hadn't seen Andrew since last week when he came with the rest of the volunteers to help with barn clean up. The animal corpses had been winched to a pickup and dragged away for burial. Charred beams were knocked down into the center of the wreckage. In spring she'd have the site bulldozed and later erect a new barn. It all depended on how much farming she and Tom would be doing, or if they decided to leave the area.

Aware that she'd been silent too long, Sarah asked, "How have you been?"

"Great. Keeping busy."

"That's good."

"I just wanted to tell you how sorry I was about the fire." Andrew's hands were in his pockets and he toed at the ground. "When is the court date?"

"Reed is out of the hospital and in jail now. The hearing is set for next month. Both Tom and I have to testify. The sheriff expects he'll get a few years of prison time."

"Well, that's good."

Just then Bonnie Samuels walked up and possessively linked her arm through Andrew's. "Hello, Sarah. So sorry about your barn. Andy and I were just saying that we should get the community involved and have a barn raising next spring, weren't we, Andy?"

"Mm-hm." Andrew blushed.

Bonnie's intentions were obvious. Although she was only twenty-two and Andrew nearly forty, bachelors were in short supply since the war. Bonnie knew a solid match when she saw one.

Bone Deep

"I'm starving. Are you ready to go join the line?" Bonnie asked Andrew, then she turned to Sarah. "You'll stick around after the barbeque for the softball game, won't you? You and your, uh, boyfriend?" Bonnie didn't wait for an answer but deftly guided Andrew away.

Sarah smiled. Bonnie would be perfect for Andrew. She would dominate him with kid gloves and he'd be content.

She looked for Tom in the crowd. He was easy to find, standing near the house, talking with Charlie Burkett. Sarah headed over to join them.

Charlie greeted her. "We were just discussing the bottom quarter and whether you'll want me to work it for you next summer. Truth is, it'd be nice to cut back on my workload and Tom here thinks he'd like to give it a try. I can teach him what needs to be done and rent out my plow and planter for you to use. What do you think?"

"It sounds perfect." Sarah imagined next spring; Tom out in the field plowing and she swollen to bursting with a new life. By her calculations the baby should be born in June. It was too much to wrap her mind around such an enormous change in her life. Suddenly all she wanted was to be at home away from all these people sneaking looks at them, whispering and wondering behind their backs.

"Tom can even help me with the late harvest if he wants to. I could afford to pay a little," Charlie added.

Tom looked as thrilled as when Sarah had offered to teach him to read. "Thank you. I'd like that. When can I start?"

Sarah was pleased at his easy rapport with Charlie. She

left them talking farming and walked around the far side of the house to get away from the crowd for a few moments. She rounded the corner of an outbuilding and surprised Shirley Brodbeck necking with her boyfriend Eric Samuels.

"Oh, excuse me!"

The young lovers pulled quickly apart. The boy jumped back and ducked his head sheepishly. Shirley sprang away from the wall Eric had her pressed up against.

"That's okay. We were just about to go back." Shirley grabbed her boyfriend's hand and they hurried toward the party.

Sarah sat down in the grass, knees drawn to her chest as she rested her forehead against them. Her mind continued to spin around thought of Tom, their future, and their child.

How dark and empty her life had been when Tom had gone missing and how she'd feared for him when he fought Reed. She pictured a hundred different moments with Tom over the past month: his face shining in the sun, his smile when he looked up at her from a book, his quiet humming when he thought she wasn't listening, his hands stroking her body slowly, his eyes telling her she was everything he wanted in the world.

She raised her face and looked off across the field. The answer was so clear she wondered what she'd been working herself up over. She loved this man, his simplicity and sweetness, and nothing else mattered. Everything else fell away.

Sarah stood, ready to hold her head high, eat barbeque and visit with her friends and neighbors as if there was nothing out of the ordinary about her choice of man. And at the end of the day she would curl up with Tom in their bed and tell him the news that he was going to be a father.

Later, as she lay beneath Tom, the heat of his body covering her and the cool breeze from the open window drying the sheen of sweat on her skin, Sarah was completely content.

He moved inside her slowly thrusting, but with no urgency, simply filling her with himself. Her hands roved up and down the planes of his back and buttocks, feeling him tense and release with each stroke.

The gentle pace was peaceful, but soon Sarah felt tension building deep inside her. It coiled lazily through her, blossoming from a general sense of desire to a throbbing need and finally an explosion that shuddered through her. She shook and moaned.

Tom made a satisfied murmuring sound and pressed a kiss to her throat. His pace increased as he pushed into her with increasing urgency. She watched his face, the frown of concentration, his parted lips as he strove toward climax. Her body clenched around his cock. She pictured the barbed wire tattoo encircling it and remembered Reed's voice in her ear asking if it scratched.

Part of her wished he'd died. He might be released from prison some day, but he could never come back from the grave. But they were safe from him for now, and he would probably never bother them again.

She dismissed thoughts of the evil man and focused on

Tom rising above her and thrusting deep as he reached his point of no return. He bucked into her hard, crying out his release then collapsed on top of her panting against her neck. She embraced him, humming into his shoulder and caressing the soft hair curling at the nape of his neck.

At last Tom rolled off to lie beside her, one arm draped across her body. She linked fingers with him, enjoying the contrast of her pale skin and his riotous color. Their hands moved together playfully, Sarah trying to pin Tom's thumb down with her own.

"I have something important to tell you," she said after a moment, bringing their joined hands down to rest on her belly. She took a deep breath. "I'm pregnant."

Tom was silent.

"I'm going to have a baby."

After a long pause, he said, "My baby?"

She turned her head on the pillow and glared at him. "Well, of course! Who else? You do understand how it works don't you?" She couldn't help her irritable tone. Her hormones were running rampant, and she'd assumed Tom would be happy at the news. Wasn't a family what he'd always wished for?

He gazed back at her with solemn eyes. "Yes, I understand but..."

"What?" She tried to read his expression. Sometimes it was so hard. A hundred thoughts were flashing through his mind, but she couldn't capture and examine even one.

"How can...?" He closed his eyes a moment then opened them to fix her with his vibrant blue gaze. "I'm glad.

We would be a family then, wouldn't we?"

"Yes."

"But will the baby be happy? When it's older and wants to have friends and be normal."

Sarah rubbed his arm. "Things may be hard right now, but the longer we live here, the more people will get used to you. Maybe by the time our child is old enough for school people won't even consider us different anymore." She said it with confidence she certainly wasn't feeling.

He reached up to tuck a strand of hair behind her ear. A slow smile curved his lips. "Should we get married then?"

She smiled back. "It might help. Do you want to marry me?"

"Yes."

"Do you love me?"

His eyes answered more eloquently than the single word that issued almost soundlessly from his lips, "Yes."

"I love you too." She rolled onto her side and kissed his lips. "I want to get married and have our baby and live together here until we're as old as the Burketts."

"I want that too." He gathered her into his arms and kissed her deeply. "I love you, Sarah."

Propping her head on one hand, she watched Tom sleep, her gaze lingering on the meticulous artwork of each design that covered his skin like a quilt. Evil as he was, she had to admit Reed was a talented artist. Tom's canvas of skin was intricately filled with dynamic color and motion.

When she'd first seen him, she'd thought there was no

pattern or reason behind the designs, but the more she looked at them, the more she felt there was a significant message just beyond her grasp. Whatever the meaning, her lover's painted skin was beautiful. *He* was beautiful, both inside and out.

A fierce wave of love swept through her. She vowed she would always show him the love he'd been denied for so many years. She had already given him her heart, her body, her home, and now she would give him the new life growing inside of her.

Together they would create the family both had always wanted.

The End

About the Author:

Whether you're a fan of contemporary, paranormal, or historical romance, you'll find something to enjoy. My style is very personal and my characters will feel like well-known friends by the time you've finished reading. I'm interested in flawed, often damaged, people who find the fulfillment they seek in one another.
Stop by my web site, http://bonniedee.com
or for future updates on my books, join my Yahoo group,
http://groups.yahoo.com/group/bonniedee/

**Read on for an excerpt from A Hearing Heart
another historical with an unusual hero.**

The heart conveys messages beyond what ears can hear.

After the death of her fiancé, Catherine Johnson, a New York schoolteacher in 1902, travels to Nebraska to teach in a one-room school and escape her sad memories. One afternoon, violence erupts in the sleepy town. Catherine saves deaf stable hand, Jim Kinney from torture by drunken thugs.

As she takes charge of his education, teaching him to read and sign, attraction grows between them. The warmth and humor in this silent man transcends the need for speech and his eyes tell her all she needs to know about his feelings for her. But the obstacles of class difference and the stigma of his handicap are almost insurmountable barriers to their growing attachment.

Will Catherine flaunt society's rules and allow herself to love again? Can Jim make his way out of poverty as a deaf man in a hearing world? And together will they beat the corrupt robber baron who has a stranglehold on the town? Romance, love and sensuality abound in this jam-packed, old-fashioned tale with plenty of heart and some deeply sensual sex.

A Hearing Heart

Broughton, Nebraska, 1901

Catherine Johnson stepped out of the general mercantile onto the wooden walkway, adjusting her mesh shopping bag on one wrist and the brown paper-wrapped parcels in her other arm. A stiff breeze cut through the fabric of her dress and twisted her long skirt around her legs. Grit scoured her cheeks and stung her eyes. At least the road wasn't muddy, but she faced a long walk back to the McPhersons' farm carrying all her purchases. She'd be glad when her stay there was over and she moved in with the Albrights in town. Shuttling from home to home was one of the more unpleasant aspects of teaching in a one-room schoolhouse.

Sometimes she wished she'd never left New York to come to Nebraska. On a Saturday afternoon in White Plains she'd be strolling along a brick path in the park with fountains and flowerbeds gracing the way. Here in Broughton she fought the ever-present wind and choking dust while her shoes tapped an uneven rhythm on the warped boards of the sidewalk.

The town was quiet for a Saturday, the street nearly empty. She was almost to the last building on Main Street, where the dusty road became prairie, when several men erupted from the saloon in front of her. The swinging doors crashed against the wall.

Catherine stumbled backward, dropping one of her packages, heart pounding

A raw-boned man with no chin and his stocky, black-bearded partner dragged a man between them. Behind them staggered a burly fellow with heavy-lidded eyes. He was shouting curses, using words Catherine had never heard. The only man in the group she recognized was the one the others gripped by the arms. He was Jim Kinney, the deaf-mute man who worked at the livery stable.

Jim glared at his captors through a fringe of dark hair. The burly man moved in front of him and plowed a fist into his stomach. The stable hand doubled over with a whoosh of air.

The skinny man hauled him upright and the bearded one punched his jaw, snapping his head to the side. Jim cried out, a hoarse, wordless sound. Bracing himself against the pair holding his arms, he kicked out with both feet at the man who'd hit him, landing a solid blow to his chest.

"Tie him up," the droopy-eyed man slurred. "Teach him some respect."

Catherine stood rooted to the spot, horrified but too shocked to react as one of the men grabbed a rope from his horse's saddle at the hitching post. When he began tying Jim's hands, she finally found her voice.

"Stop it! Stop!" She dropped her parcels and bag on the sidewalk and ran toward them. "Leave him alone!"

For a second, Jim's dark eyes met hers, and then the men dragged him out to the street, whooping in drunken glee

A Hearing Heart

and ignoring Catherine as if she was voiceless.

"Stop!" she yelled in frustration, her hands clenching helplessly at her sides.

The black-bearded man blocked her way, and she pushed past him, the sour stench of sweat and alcohol wrinkling her nose.

The leader mounted his horse and wrapped the end of the rope around the pommel of his saddle. Jim struggled to free his hands until the rope stretched taut and jerked him forward, forcing him to keep pace with the horse. The rider kneed his mount and it moved from a walk to a trot.

Jim ran behind, stumbling as he tried to keep on his feet.

Catherine screamed for help. A few men came from the saloon while others stepped out of stores along the street.

"Help!" she cried again, panic swelling in her chest. "Somebody help him."

Jim couldn't keep up with the speed of the horse. He tripped, fell and was dragged along the ground. Spooked by the creature on its heels, the horse whinnied and plunged ahead. A cloud of dust from its hooves concealed the body bumping over the ruts behind it.

The rider pulled the horse's head up, turned and rode back toward where his companions stood laughing and shouting encouragement.

People emerging from the barbershop, the mercantile and feed store all stood watching. No one was going to interfere, risking the drunken men's anger.

The horse cantered toward Catherine. Without a

thought beyond stopping the stable hand's torture, she ran into the road, waving her arms and shouting. The animal reared on its hind legs, dumping its rider to the ground. For a moment all she could see was hooves flailing and the chestnut body rising high above her. How very tall a horse was when standing on two legs. The inane thought flashed in her mind before the animal came down on all fours.

She seized the bridle and her fingers grazed its warm jaw. The horse blew hay-scented breath into her face with a soft chuffing sound.

"Sh. Easy. Easy," she crooned, stroking its neck. She moved alongside and reached for the rope tied to the pommel. Even standing on her toes with her chest pressed against the horse's heaving flank she could barely reach it, and the knot was so tight she couldn't loosen it.

Catherine glanced at Jim's dusty body sprawled in the road, and the horse's rider staggering to his feet, cursing as he brushed off his clothes.

Now that the crisis was past, a couple of men from the feed store came out to the street and grabbed the leader of the thugs, while someone else ran to get the deputy. A few patrons of the tavern collared the other two roughnecks. Mr. Murdoch, the saloonkeeper knelt in the road beside Jim and untied his wrists.

Catherine walked over to the prone body of the stable hand and watched Murdoch feel his limbs for broken bones.

"Is he alive?" She squatted beside the dust-covered body, her skirt pooling around her. The man's eyes were closed and blood seeped from abrasions on his dirt-streaked face.

"He's unconscious, but I think he'll be all right. Damn! If only he'd kept out of their way," Murdoch said.

"He needs the doctor."

"Already sent someone to get him."

Catherine pulled her handkerchief from her sleeve and dabbed at the blood on Jim's forehead. "What happened?"

"Drunken fools called for another round. Shirley was tending another table so they shouted at Jim to get their drinks. Of course, he couldn't hear 'em. He's there to push a broom, not wait tables. They started yelling, grabbed him and dragged him outside."

Catherine bit back her question of why it had taken him so long to come to Jim's aid. Pushing back a lock of the man's dark hair, she examined the wound at his temple. "I thought Mr. Kinney worked at the livery stable."

"Works there too. Has a room back of the stables. Christ! Where's the damn doc? Pardon the language."

A young woman ran up to them, her skirts held high enough to show striped stockings all the way to her knees. Her red hair straggled from the bun in back to frame her round, red-cheeked face. The neckline of her dress revealed most of her bosom, which rose and fell as she panted. "Doc's out on a call, Mr. Murdoch. Is he okay?"

"Damn! Hope to hell there ain't anything broken. Guess all we can do is carry him back to his room."

Several men had gathered around, and three of them lifted Jim's body. He groaned, and his eyes opened, his gaze focusing on Catherine.

She smiled. "It's all right. You'll be all right."

He blinked, but she didn't know if he'd understood. She'd only seen the man once or twice since she'd moved here. People said he was slow as well as deaf and mute.

Walking beside the men carrying him, she kept her gaze locked on his in an attempt to offer encouragement. The eyes that stared back at her were focused and intelligent. She could almost see his thoughts busily flickering in them, but with no voice to give substance those thoughts remained locked inside. Catherine realized he wasn't mentally impaired at all.

The men carried him through the doors of the livery stable, and Catherine lost eye contact with Jim. Her stomach churned and her nerves jangled, unsurprising since a rearing horse had nearly trampled her. The deputy would probably have questions for her as the main witness of the altercation, but for now she was intent on seeing what she could do to help Jim Kinney. She followed the men into the livery.

* * * *

His body ached in a thousand places. Every bone hurt. Every inch of exposed skin was shredded. He felt like he'd been dragged down the street behind a horse. Jim smiled at the sarcastic thought, then groaned as one of the men carrying him jarred his right side.

Three faces hovered above him. Murdoch frowned. His mouth moved beneath his handlebar moustache as he said something to John Walker from the hardware store. Jim recognized the third man from the feed store. Their faces were strained with the effort of carrying him and their fiercely gripping hands hurt like hell. He wished they'd set him down and let him get himself back to his room. Even if he had to crawl it would be less painful.

Jim glanced past Walker, who was carrying his legs, and tried to catch another glimpse of the schoolteacher. She must've left.

He wondered if any of his bones were broken, wondered if someone was getting the doctor, and how he'd pay the man. How soon would he be able to work again? If his body failed him, he was in trouble. That's why he always took good care of himself, careful to keep healthy and steer clear of dangerous situations. From a lifetime of practice, he'd become adept at avoiding drunks or bullies who wanted to show their manliness with their fists and found him an easy target.

But today he hadn't been alert. He'd been thinking about Shirley Mae and what she'd done for him the previous night. He'd only paid for a hand job. It was all he could afford, but he was desperate for something more than his own touch. Shirley had given him a blowjob for free. She'd pointed to the rhinestone comb in her hair, the one he'd found one day while sweeping the bar and returned to her, then she'd bent her head and taken his cock in her mouth. With that memory in mind, he hadn't even been aware of the three drunken men until they grabbed him.

Now Walker and the other men were maneuvering Jim through the narrow doorway of his room. He gritted his teeth to keep from crying out as they jostled his body. When they laid him on his cot, he exhaled in relief.

His small room was crowded with bodies, but soon all

of the men left except his two bosses, Murdoch and Rasmussen, the livery owner. They spoke together a moment. He couldn't see their lips and was too tired to read them anyway. His eyes drifted closed.

They opened again at the pressure of Murdoch's hand on his shoulder. He explained slowly that the doctor was out on a call, patted Jim's shoulder and left the room.

Mr. Rasmussen sat on the edge of the bed, pushed his glasses up his nose and frowned, a sure sign he didn't know what he was doing. He might be able to wrap a horse's strained leg, but what did he know about people? Jim inhaled a deep breath and pain pierced his side. Something was wrong with his ribs. He gestured to his side, letting Rasmussen know. The man nodded and began unbuttoning what was left of his shredded shirt.

A movement in the doorway caught Jim's attention. The schoolteacher stood framed there in her blue and white-flowered dress with her daffodil-colored hair. A faint scent of lily-of-the-valley perfume wafted to him. She was like a flower garden filling the dark, stuffy room.

She looked at Rasmussen before entering the room. Only a few paces brought her to the edge of Jim's bed.

He couldn't stop staring at her like the idiot everyone thought he was. The sight of her fresh, feminine form in his dingy room was unbelievable, besides which he was dizzy and near passing out from the pain throbbing in his head. His gaze fastened on her lips.

"What can I do?" she asked Rasmussen.

The stableman turned toward her so Jim couldn't see

A Hearing Heart

his reply. Miss Johnson nodded and left the room. He felt pain that had nothing to do with his injured body as she disappeared from view.

Rasmussen lifted Jim's torso, peeled off his long-sleeved shirt and undershirt, and lowered him back onto the bed. Colors and lights flashed in front of his eyes and the edges of his vision grew dark. Oh God, his worst nightmare was coming true. He would be blinded from the blow to his head and left totally helpless. His pulse beat wildly as panic surged through him. He gasped for breath and could see again. Rasmussen was frowning at him.

"Where does it hurt?"

Jim indicated his head.

"You'll be all right. I'll fix you up."

How the hell do you know? You can barely tend the horses! Jim nodded, his jaw clenching at the pain.

Suddenly the teacher was back. She carried a bucket of water in one hand and some clean rags from the tack room in the other. Offering them to Rasmussen, she glanced at Jim. Her eyes widened at the sight of his bare torso and she quickly looked away.

Rasmussen rose, indicating she should take his seat and wash the blood and dust from Jim's face and body. He was going to get liniment. The teacher looked after Rasmussen as he walked from the room, her mouth open as if to protest, then she closed it and turned back to Jim. Her smile was tense.

"You. Read. Lips?" She shaped each word carefully.

He nodded.

"I'm going to clean you." She sat on the cot next to

him, her warm hip pressed against his. She dipped one of the rags, squeezed it out and leaned over him to sponge off the blood at his temple. The cloth was cold but it felt good.

He let his eyes drift closed and submitted to the pressure of the wet cloth dabbing his face. She held his chin in her other hand as she bathed his forehead, cheek and neck. Her skin was soft and the scent of lilies much stronger with her so close. Beneath the flowers, he could smell her body, a secret, womanly aroma.

Jim opened his eyes, watching her bend to rinse the rag in the bucket. Her sun-colored hair was pulled back into a bun at the nape of her neck. Tendrils of hair curled around her face. Two perfectly arched, light brown eyebrows were knitted in a frown of concentration over sky-blue eyes. Her tongue darted out, wetting her lips, and his heart jolted in his chest.

Turning back to him, she began patting again, this time on the bloody abrasion on his shoulder. The pink blush rising in her cheeks told him she was uncomfortable touching him. A lady didn't do such things to a strange man. He couldn't stop watching her eyes even though she refused to meet his gaze. He'd never seen eyes so blue.

All he knew about her was that she was the new teacher. He'd seen her around town a few times. Once, at the mercantile he'd watched as she laughed and talked with a little girl. Her smile and the sweet affection she'd shown the child had made him smile. He'd also seen her walking to and from the schoolhouse. But he didn't know her name. No one had said it in front of him and he couldn't ask. There was no reason for him to know it. Yet now he was desperate to have a word for her, a shape of the lips that meant *her*, even if he couldn't imagine what the word sounded like.

Jim touched her hand and she finally looked at him. He pointed at her and raised his eyebrows, requesting her name.

"Catherine Johnson." Her hand touched her chest and her lips moved slowly over each syllable.

Mimicking her, he felt her name with his thrusting tongue and moving lips. Without knowing the sound, he'd never forget the shapes. Memorization came easy to him.

Jim nodded and smiled, accepting the gift of her name.

Find more about A Hearing Heart at BonnieDee.com

Look for These Titles from Bonnie Dee

Contemporaries:
Four Kisses
Serious Play (w/Summer Devon)
Hired for Her Pleasure
Finding Home (w/Lauren Baker)
Opposites Attract
Butterfly Unpinned (w/Laura Bacchi)
The Final Act
The Valentine Effect
Awakening

Historicals:
Captive Bride
Blackberry Pie
Perfecting Amanda
The Countess Takes a Lover
The Countess Lends a Hand
The Gypsy's Vow
Bone Deep
A Hearing Heart
Liberating Lucius

Paranormal and Fantasy:
After the End
Dead Country
Magical Menages: Shifters' Captive
Magical Menages: Vampires' Consort
Fairytale Fantasies: Cinderella Unmasked (w/Marie Treanor)
Fairytale Fantasies: Demon Lover (w/Marie Treanor)
Fairytale Fantasies: Awakening Beauty (w/Marie Treanor)
The Warrior's Gift
Shifter, P.I.
Like Clockwork
Evolving Man

The Thief and the Desert Flower
Empath
Dream Across Time
Rock Hard
Mirror Image (w/Mima)
The Straw Man
Terran Realm: Measure of a Man
Terran Realm: Fruits of Betrayal

M/m all genres:
Undeniable Magnetism
Cage Match
Star Flyer
Jungle Heat
Ignite!
Seducing Stephen
The Gentleman and the Rogue (w/Summer Devon)
The Nobleman and the Spy (w/Summer Devon)
House of Mirrors (w/Summer Devon)
The Psychic and the Sleuth (w/Summer Devon)

Anthologies:
Seasons of Love
Prime Passions
Hot Summer Nights
Heat Wave: print anthology
Strangers in the Night: print anthology
Gifted: print anthology
Red Velvet & Absinthe
The Handsome Prince
Beyond Desire
Secrets, Volume 23
Lust: Erotic Fantasies for Women
Best Women's Erotica
Got a Minute?: Sixty Second Erotic

Made in the USA
Lexington, KY
02 November 2016